FIGHTING FOR THE FORBIDDEN

SUBMITTING TO MY STEPBROTHER
BOOK 7

M. FRANCIS HASTINGS

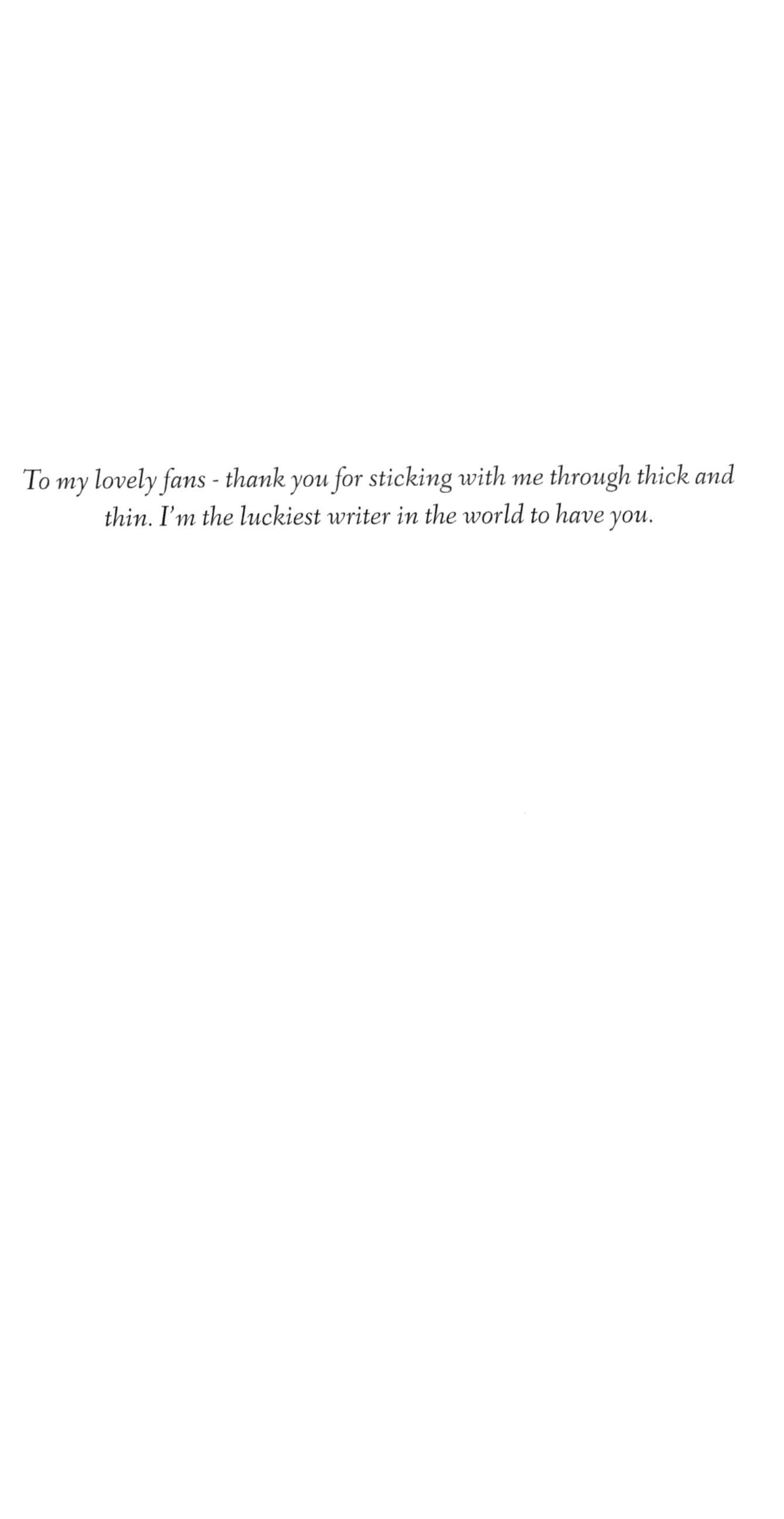

To my lovely fans - thank you for sticking with me through thick and thin. I'm the luckiest writer in the world to have you.

CONTENTS

ONE

THERE WILL BE BLOOD

Will

The first thing I realized when I woke up was that McKenzie was not beside me.

This was not acceptable.

I touched her side of the bed, which still had an indent from her body, hoping it might manifest her. But no, she was gone.

My head throbbing with a horrible headache, I sat up. I didn't bother calling her name. I knew in my bones she wasn't in the bathroom or the closet. I could feel her absence as though my heart had been torn from my body.

I swung my legs over the side of the bed, bracing myself on the bedside dresser as I stood and fought a wave of dizziness. Whatever Marvin—or, rather, Bran—had given me had some nasty side-effects. I wanted to throw up.

But I wasn't willing to sit in the bathroom with my head in the toilet while McKenzie was God only knew where.

I weaved my way to the door and tried the handle again. It was locked. No surprise there. I balled up my fist and banged hard on it. "MARVIN!!!" I bellowed.

The door unlocked, and Bran's loyal minion stood in the doorway. "Mr. Masterson, how can I hel—?"

I punched him in the face. I was beyond finished with Bran's games, Bran's house, Bran's minions... anything to do with Bran.

Marvin cried out in surprise, holding his eye. I grabbed him by the starched shirt front and drew him close so we were nose-to-nose. "Now, you listen to me. If you don't want your jaw wired shut at the ER, I suggest you tell me where McKenzie is. Right now!"

"B-But, sir, I have orders—" he jibbered.

I pulled my fist back and took aim.

He wasn't as stupid as I thought. Pointing down the hall, he said, "The guesthouse. They're in the guesthouse."

They? My blood ran cold. I shoved Marvin in front of me, keeping a hand on his shoulder in case he tried to escape. "Show me."

He nodded vigorously and quickly guided me through the mansion out to a paved walk that led to the guesthouse.

I forced him to take me all the way to the front door. There was no way I was going to be defeated by another lock. "Open it," I ordered him.

Marvin pressed in a code with shaking fingers.

The keypad turned red and made an angry sound.

"Sorry, I must have put it in wrong," he said, the look in his eyes telling me he'd done it on purpose.

Red rage struck me like a bolt of lightning. I grabbed the back of his head and slammed his nose into the door.

There was a loud crunch, and he squealed.

"Now, I'm hoping I don't have to ask you again," I whispered dangerously in his ear.

"No, sir. Sorry, sir," he groaned and began punching in the numbers again.

A loud scream echoed from inside the house.

Marvin stopped typing, his jaw dropping in surprise.

I tightened my fingers in his hair. "Don't just fucking stand there, open the goddamn door!"

"Yes, sir!" He typed frantically, and the keypad finally turned green, and the door unlocked.

I shoved him aside and yanked the door open, panic making it hard to breathe at the same time it spurred me on. "McKenzie?!" I yelled, glancing around frantically.

"Will!"

My gaze snapped to the kitchen where McKenzie was sitting on the floor, bruised. Clearly, she'd been beaten.

Bran Lockwood the Fifth was a dead man.

I ran to her side, gathering her carefully in my arms. "Where's Bran?" I asked, trying not to sound harsh.

"I-I don't know. I stabbed him, and he ran away," she hiccuped. "He... he hurt me. He wanted to r-rape me. I fought him, but he was so much stronger. He kept hitting me."

"Oh, honeybee." The part of me that was boiling over with anger wanted to go find Bran and tear his dick off, wherever his cowardly ass was hiding. But I couldn't leave McKenzie alone.

"He didn't, though. He didn't rape me." She sounded particularly proud of that fact.

"He hurt you. That's what matters to me." I kissed her hair. "We're going to take you to the hospital to get you looked at, okay? It looks like he hit you in the head a few times, and I want to make sure you don't have a concussion."

McKenzie clung to me, pressing herself against my bare chest, her arms around my neck. "How do we get out of here? He still has our car." Her breath hitched. "I just want to go home."

"I know, honeybee. I know." I carefully pulled her into my lap.

Marvin was hovering, and I speared him with a cold gaze. "Get our fucking car."

"Yes, sir," he replied, looking at McKenzie and deflating. "I didn't know things would go this far, sir. I do apologize."

"The. Car." I gently peeled her off me so I could stand and scoop her up in my arms.

I didn't like the way she groaned.

"Dizzy?" I asked worriedly, my own dizziness kept at bay by sheer adrenaline.

She nodded, then groaned again. "Maybe nodding wasn't a good plan," she said.

Marvin scampered off, and I carried her out of the guesthouse, following the path to the front of the mansion where, blessedly, the McLaren was waiting.

"Where is Bran?" I asked Marvin as he handed me the keys.

"I don't know, sir. And that's the honest truth. I didn't see him on the way to the garage," he said.

I set McKenzie carefully in the passenger seat. "When you do see him, tell him I said his days are numbered." I went to the driver's side and got in.

"Are you sure you should be driving, sir? The sedative in your tea was very powerful," Marvin fretted.

"I don't trust anyone else here to drive us. Not even you," I said. Then I threw the car in gear and headed down the drive.

Marvin had the good sense to make sure the gate was open, and I barreled through it, not wanting to risk being caught in that hellhole one more minute.

"Do you think he's dead?" McKenzie asked softly.

"Bran? I sure as hell hope so," I replied, navigating around Lake Minnetonka to get us to the nearest ER.

"It was just a paring knife," she mumbled. "I'm not sure I got him good enough to kill him."

"Then I'll finish the job later," I promised darkly.

She didn't answer. I glanced over to see she'd passed out.

"Shit!" Keeping one eye on the road, I gave her a shake. "Honey-bee, you can't go to sleep yet. We have to see the doctor first."

McKenzie didn't respond.

Panic set in, and I floored it, almost hoping we'd get pulled over. However, no police showed up between Lake Minnetonka and the ER at North Memorial Hospital.

I screeched to a stop at the ER doors and leapt out of the car.

A rather annoyed woman in scrubs came striding out. "Sir, you can't park here—"

"My fiancée was beaten, and now she's passed out and won't wake up," I said frantically. "You have to get her help!"

The woman's eyes narrowed. "Are you telling me you beat your fiancée unconscious, sir?"

"No—fuck, woman, does that really matter right now?! She needs help!" I shouted.

"I see. Please stand aside. I will assess her and see if she needs immediate help. We're rather full up today." The woman pushed me aside while I stared openmouthed at her.

She took McKenzie's pulse then took out a penlight and flashed it in her eyes.

Meanwhile, I tried very hard to stop myself from making a scene.

"I believe she has a concussion. I'll call for a gurney, and we'll get her into a CT scan right away. Unfortunately, you can't accompany her, sir. You will need to speak with the police first," the woman said firmly.

"Fine. Here's the keys to my car. Move it if you want. I'm not running away," I responded, dropping the keys into her palm.

She nodded, and, when the gurney arrived, so did security. She gave my keys to one of the guards then had a murmured conversation with him while four people in scrubs gingerly moved McKenzie to the gurney and began wheeling her away.

I watched her go, feeling as though I was being ripped in two. But I didn't want anything getting in the way of her being treated. Especially not some futile tantrum on my part.

"Sir? Please come with us. The police should be here shortly," a security guard said, firmly taking my arm.

While another security guard drove my car away, I turned to the one who had me by the arm. "I'm going to need a drug test," I informed him.

He frowned at me. "You think being high is going to save you from being charged with assault?"

I took a deep breath and mentally counted backward from fifty. "No. I was knocked out so I couldn't stop someone else from assaulting my fiancée. I'm still not a hundred percent, and I want to be when McKenzie wakes up. I might need medicine."

"You... were knocked out so another man could assault your fiancée?" the guard repeated.

"Yes. That's what happened." I walked with him to a small office where he sat me down at a table.

"The police will be here soon, but I'll call someone up from the lab for a tox screen," the security guard said, sounding dubious.

Even though he doubted my story, I was glad he was at least doing what I asked. "Thank you."

He nodded and spoke into his walkie-talkie, summoning a young lady in a white coat to come take my blood. When she left, the police arrived.

"Mr. Masterson," they said without even asking for ID. "We had a call from Mr. Ike Freeborn. Apparently, you and Mr. Bran Lockwood had an altercation?"

So that's how they're going to spin it. "If I say yes, does that mean McKenzie Kent is absolved of any wrongdoing?"

The officer blinked at me. "Mr. Freeborn told us there had been a drunken misunderst—"

"He misunderstood that his fist did not belong in my fiancée's face," I said angrily. "That's the only 'misunderstanding' there was."

"Is that why you stabbed him?" the officer asked.

"Like I said, if I say yes, does that get McKenzie Kent off the hook?" I replied.

"Are you... trying to tell me that Miss Kent stabbed Mr. Lockwood after he assaulted her?" the officer said shrewdly.

I nodded. "But if she's going to get into any sort of trouble for it, I will swear under oath that I did it."

"That's... not really something you're supposed to do, Mr. Masterson. That's called perjury." The officer who was speaking to me sat down across from me while the other silently guarded the door. "So, what I'm hearing is that Miss Kent stabbed Mr. Lockwood in self-defense."

"Yes." I folded my hands on top of the table. "But, as I said before...."

"You'll swear under oath that you did it if it will help Miss Kent avoid any consequences," the officer said. "Yes, I understand. Where were you when the altercation happened?"

I scowled at the table. "I was drugged."

"You were drugged?" he echoed. "How do you know you were drugged?"

"I passed out, and I hadn't had anything to drink but tea with a sedative in it, or so Mr. Lockwood's lackey told me," I said. "But I just had my blood taken for a tox screen, so I suppose we'll both find out what they gave me."

He turned to the other officer. "Make sure they put a rush on that, Edwards."

Edwards poked his head outside the door and spoke with security.

"I'll have to question Miss Kent. Where is she?" the officer asked.

"Mr. Lockwood beat her unconscious. I don't know where she is right now. They won't let me see her until I've resolved matters with you," I said.

"That's just a precaution, sir. We don't know that it wasn't *you* who beat her. Yet." He sounded sympathetic. "I know this must be torture. I'm sorry."

I raked a hand through my hair. "I honestly don't care what you need to do as long as I'm there when she wakes up. I don't want her to be alone."

"We... really do need to question her before you can see her," he apologized.

"No matter what my tox screen says?" I sighed.

"No matter what your tox screen says," he confirmed.

I groaned and rubbed my hands over my face. "This is a nightmare."

"I'll personally ensure that Miss Kent does not wake up alone. And that you can be reunited with her just as soon as we get her side of the story," he said. "Don't worry about—"

The door opened, and a woman with a stride and confidence that told me she was a doctor walked in. "Officer Pence. I was just given the results of Mr. Masterson's tox screen."

"That's excellent," he said. "What were they?"

"Mr. Masterson, please sign this waiver so that I can give the results to the police." The doctor laid a form in front of me.

I barely read it. I signed my name and handed it back.

The doctor placed the form on her clipboard, then turned to Officer Pence. "Judging by Mr. Masterson's bloodwork, we have determined he ingested a large amount of phenobarbital."

TWO

A REALLY BIG HEADACHE

McKenzie

Light stabbed my eyes, and I tried to close them again, but someone was holding my eyelid open.

"Come on back to us, McKenzie," a kind female voice said. "You had quite a knock to the noggin. I need to make sure you're okay."

I licked my dry lips. "Will...."

"He's with the police, love. They need to ask you a few questions before we can let him in," the woman said with the same even patience.

That woke me up. "Police?" I wanted to say more but started coughing instead.

"Mitchell, could you get some water?" the doctor asked.

At least I assumed she was a doctor. Her hair was pulled back in a ponytail, and she wore a white coat.

Mitchell, dressed in scrubs, trotted off and came back with a mug with a straw in it. "Here you go, Dr. Allen."

She maneuvered the straw into my mouth, and I drank greedily. I hadn't realized how thirsty I was!

"Why is Will with the police?" I finally managed to ask.

"Well...." Dr. Allen patted my hand. "When someone comes in, beaten like this, our first assumption is always that it was their partner because that's the most common thing to have happened. Mr. Masterson has basically cleared all that up. The police just need to hear from you so that we can make certain we are doing our due diligence in protecting your safety."

"Will didn't do anything to me!" I insisted, my head ringing at how loud my voice was in my ears. "It was Bran Lockwood!"

"Shh, yes love. We know. Mr. Masterson was drugged, and we have a tox screen to show it. This is really just a formality." She reached over and slowly brought the head of my bed up so I was sitting up more. "I can tell them they can come in and interview you."

"Yes, please do," I replied. "I want Will in here with me."

She nodded and went to the door.

Two uniformed police officers walked in.

"Hello, Miss Kent. My name is Officer Pence, and this is my colleague, Officer Edwards," the shorter of the two said. "Might we have a quick word?"

"Please," I said. "I want Will here as soon as possible."

"Of course." Officer Pence approached the bed while Officer Edwards hung back by Mitchell, Dr. Allen, and the door. Officer Pence pulled up a chair. "How are you feeling?"

"I have a bad headache," I admitted. "And I'm a bit dizzy.... How's Will? The doctor says he was drugged."

"He was." Officer Pence winced sympathetically. "And honestly, I wish he'd gotten an ambulance instead of driving here. On what he was given, that could have been a very tragic decision, indeed."

I shrugged and regretted it, my world swimming. "He got us out of there. That was the main thing."

"Yes. I have some questions for Mr. Lockwood." Officer Pence didn't look happy.

Good.

"Bran hit me. He was trying to rape me, and I wouldn't cooperate," I said.

He was silent for a moment. "Was he... successful? Should we order a rape kit? That is entirely your choice, of course, I'm just considering the evidence we can collect against him—"

"He wasn't successful. He didn't even get my panties off, thank God." I shuddered. "He tried to bribe his way into my pants. When that didn't work, he grabbed me and started hitting me when I fought back."

"I've had officers dispatched to his estate," he informed me. "So far, Mr. Lockwood is being seen by his private doctor for a rather nasty stab wound."

My shoulders drooped. "He's not dead?"

Officer Pence grimaced. "No."

"I suppose you can't add 'unfortunately' to that because of your job," I said bitterly.

"You'd be right about that. How did he end up getting stabbed?" he asked.

"I stuck my hand in the knife drawer in the kitchen while he was chasing me around the island and grabbed what I could. A paring knife *unfortunately*. I slashed him, then stabbed him in the chest. He said he was going to kill me," I explained.

"And you defended yourself," he said.

I raised my chin proudly. "Yes sir, I did."

"Brave girl." He began to stand. "I see no reason to keep Mr. Masterson holed up in an office any longer. I think he'll be very happy to see you. He's been falling all over himself trying to say he stabbed Mr. Lockwood if it will get you out of trouble, but I don't think that will be necessary. I know this might all get swept under the rug because... that's what tends to happen when very rich people are involved... but I don't see you getting into any trouble for it."

"You don't think Bran's going to be arrested?" I asked.

Officer Pence sighed. "No, Miss Kent. I don't. I just want to be honest with you. I'm very sorry for your ordeal, but I think things will probably end right here."

"Oh." I looked down at my hands, which had an IV and pulse monitor attached to them. "I suppose I shouldn't be surprised. Thanks for being honest and not getting my hopes up."

"You take care. I'll have Mr. Masterson brought in." He left with Officer Edwards, Mitchell, and the doctor. I could hear them muttering in the hallway, though I couldn't understand what was said.

The door swung open not two minutes later, and I sat up straighter, straining to see Will around the curtain.

It was not Will.

"McKenzie." Ike Freeborn waltzed in like he owned the wing. Maybe Masterson did? "I'm so sorry to see you like this. What a terrible misunderstanding you and Bran must have had."

"Go away. I already know nobody's going to listen to me if I try to press charges," I muttered, waving him off.

Instead, Ike sat down in the chair Officer Pence had just vacated. "True. But that doesn't mean there won't be consequences. He's a very silly boy if he thinks Mr. Masterson will simply let this go."

"One, he's at least thirty, so that 'boys-will-be-boys' bullshit isn't going to fly," I said with a scowl. "Two, Bran seems to think he's untouchable because he's Bran Lockwood *the Fifth*."

"Yes. That's what makes him truly silly. He can peg as many numbers on the end of his name as he wants. Or pad his wallet with as many dollar signs as inflate his ego. But he doesn't know what real power is." Ike smiled.

I'd never seen him look so dangerous, and it chilled me to the bone.

"He's about to find out," he added.

"O-Okay, that's good," I said with a swallow.

He handed me my water. "Drink up. We need you healthy. I do think we will need to postpone the engagement arrangements until you're looking better. Make-up will be a definite necessity over the next few weeks. And it is, of course, completely inappropriate for Bran to host your engagement party now, so we'll have to find another suitable venue. But these are things you don't need to worry about. You just get well."

I cautiously sipped my water. "What is Mr. Masterson going to do to him?"

"Hm? Oh, something painful and creative, I assure you. We haven't worked out all the details yet, but he has been apprised of the situation. We are both quite impressed with how scrappy you are." He chuckled. "You have more than a bit of your parents in you."

"Yeah, I do come from scrappy," I agreed. I hated Ike. I hated him like hell. But I also sensed in him the kind of darkness that could make Bran shit himself, and I wanted that to happen. I wanted to see that happen. So maybe, just right now, Ike was an ally in that particular quest?

The curtain rustled, and I looked up. It was all I could do not to burst into tears, which I didn't want to do in front of Ike. "Will!"

"Will, so good of you to join us," Ike said.

He ignored Ike and went around to the other side of the bed. Mindful of my cords and tubing, Will slid onto the bed and wrapped his arms around me. He was still in his swim trunks, though they had gotten him a T-shirt, while I was in a hospital gown. It was almost comical.

"Your grandfather sends his best and has also asked me to assure you that Bran will be dealt with," Ike continued as though reading off a grocery list. "I've already told McKenzie that the engagement arrangements are off until she's healed up some. The cameras, you know. Optics, etc. You understand. There is a gallery opening Thursday evening—"

"Cancel it," Will interrupted flatly.

Ike paused. "I will arrange an excellent make-up artist for McKenzie—"

"*Cancel it*," Will repeated.

With an annoyed sigh, Ike took out his phone and began

smashing his fingers across the screen. "That is most disappointing, Will, but I'm sure your grandfather will understand."

"What is being done?" Will asked, looking over me to spear Ike with an intense gaze.

I would not have wanted to be on the receiving end of that look.

Ike, to my shock, actually shifted uncomfortably. "Your grandfather has not yet instructed me, but I expect I will know within the next two days." He recovered himself and mused with a slight smile. "Maybe he'll want to finish the job of twisting Bran's balls off."

"Finish the job?" Will asked.

I blushed. "I sort of grabbed and ripped."

Will looked down at me and grinned. "You did an impressive amount of damage."

"Yeah, well, maybe he'll think twice before coming after me again." I grumbled.

An expression he must have inherited from his grandfather crossed Will's face, and I shrank back a little. "He won't be coming after you again." His words were cold, measured. A promise, not a threat.

"We can definitely agree on that," Ike said, almost as cold.

"I almost feel sorry for him," I murmured. "I don't think he quite understands what he's dealing with."

"Who, dear. He doesn't understand *who* he's dealing with. And, after all these years, he should," Ike corrected me.

"Will we get to see it happen?" Will asked what I was thinking.

Ike chuckled. "In your shoes, I'd want the same thing. We'll see. Like I said, I need to work out the details with your grandfather."

With a nod, Will went back to cuddling me. "Thank you, Ike," he said after a long pause.

Ike's eyebrows shot up, and his smile widened. "You're welcome, Will. You see? When we all work together, great things can be accomplished."

"Yes," Will answered softly. "I see."

THREE
GREAT THINGS

Will

I'm pretty sure the staff were not happy with me crawling into McKenzie's hospital bed with her. I was just as sure I didn't care. Feeling her breathe next to me gave me a greater sense of peace than I'd ever experienced, especially after everything that had happened.

She stroked my hair, and I held her around the waist, my face buried in her neck.

"Mr. Masterson," Dr. Allen said with failing patience after what felt like minutes but must have been hours, judging by the sun setting through the window. "I must insist you push fluids. We need to make sure all those drugs get out of your system."

I just frowned at her.

McKenzie tugged on my hair. "Will, it's important. I don't want you to get sick."

With a sigh, I reluctantly sat up and accepted the ice water they gave me, sipping it through a straw.

"Your friend, Mr. Freeborn, may be quite stubborn, but I am, too. If you want to continue to be curled up like that, you need to follow my advice," Dr. Allen said primly. "Do you understand?'

"Yes, Doctor," I grumped, still sipping my water.

"Good. Now, since Miss Kent, thankfully, has sustained only a mild concussion, we will keep her overnight for observation and then send you both home in the morning. We could send you home now, but Mr. Freeborn was most insistent and I believe made a call to the hospital director," the doctor sighed.

I winced. "Sorry about that. He's... an insistent kind of man."

"Yes, well, you will both be receiving excellent overnight care, I can guarantee that. Get some rest. I'll check on you again in the morning." She turned to go, muttering under her breath about rich people always getting what they want.

I couldn't correct her, so I just pretended not to hear.

"Should we go?" McKenzie asked me. "I don't want to be taking up a bed if someone else needs it."

"Ike would probably have someone stop us at the door." I offered her my water.

She shook her finger at me. "That's for you. You drink that whole thing, William Masterson the Third, *and* ask for more!"

"Fine, fine." I sucked down more water. "Where's your water?"

"It's over there. Plus, I have an IV," she pointed out.

In all honesty, I didn't want to leave her to have to pee. Luckily, we both fell asleep before that happened.

Nurses came in every hour, on the hour, to check on us. When McKenzie was helped to the bathroom, I took the opportunity to use the one out in the hall.

I saw Ike's bodyguard sitting in a chair outside our room. He looked at me sharply as I passed.

"Relax. I'm not running away. Just going to the restroom," I said.

He nodded and went back to looking intimidating.

It was Ike's bodyguard who pulled around to the exit in the McLaren when McKenzie and I were discharged the next day. He was silent and stoic but also an excellent driver, it turned out.

I'd had so much water at McKenzie's insistence that I felt as though I was floating. But I was much more concerned about her.

"Are you sure you're feeling well enough to go home?" I asked her for the thousandth time while we were chauffeured back to the house.

"Yes. I want to find out if Gwendolyn is okay," she replied anxiously.

Gwendolyn. I'd completely forgotten about her.

"Miss Evers is resting in her apartment. Mr. Freeborn took the liberty of assigning a bodyguard to her," Ike's bodyguard said.

Of course, he was listening. For once, I was glad. "Is she okay?" I asked.

He nodded. "He slapped her across the face, leaving a bruise, but that was the extent of it. Mr. Freeborn says he will ensure the Lockwood Estate issues a handsome settlement."

"That *asshole,*" McKenzie swore.

I gave her an incredulous look. She'd been beaten within an inch of her life and nearly raped, and she was more angry that Gwendolyn got slapped once?!

But then, I knew she wouldn't be McKenzie if she didn't feel that way. I kissed her bruised forehead gently. "You have a big heart."

"Don't tell me you weren't worried, too," she said, lacing her fingers through mine.

"I... honestly forgot she even existed after I saw what he'd done to you," I responded, not wanting to lie. "Not... one of my finer moments, I'm sure, but...."

She patted my cheek. "We'll work on that. I think if I'd seen you on the floor after Bran beat *you* up, I'd have forgotten she existed, too."

I relaxed, feeling a little absolved of my guilt. "I'm glad she's okay, for the most part. We'll have to have her over when everyone's feeling better."

"I'm hoping the settlement sets her up for life so she doesn't have to keep putting up with bullshit from creepy guys," she said.

I nodded my agreement. "I hope so, too."

"It's just... she was in that position because of me. Bran wanted to use her to get into my pants," she told me sadly.

"No, honeybee. It's not your fault. It's mine. I should have dealt with Bran years ago. It's his obsession with me that made this all happen," I assured her, feeling like crap. I believed every word.

McKenzie squeezed my hand. "There's no way you could have known he'd take it that far. I mean, he didn't come off as a lunatic at the charity event."

"True." I had to concede the point. Bran had seemed mostly sane at Comunidades en Común's auction. A bit of a voyeur, but mostly sane. "Maybe he's on drugs?" I speculated.

"I had that thought, too. Not that it excuses his behavior." She snuggled into my shoulder. "I'm glad we're finally going home. And that we don't have to see him ever again."

"I'm afraid you will be seeing him, Miss Kent," Ike's bodyguard chimed in.

We both stared at him. "What?"

"At the gallery opening on Thursday." He didn't take his eyes from the road once.

"We're not going to the gallery opening. I told Ike," I said angrily.

He smiled slightly, and it came off as rather sinister. "Mr. Freeborn insists. He said you wouldn't want to miss it."

I looked at McKenzie. She looked at me.

"Is Bran being punished at the gallery opening?" I asked.

His smile widened. "He is."

I nodded. "Then I think we will attend."

"Mr. Freeborn thought you might see things his way," he chuckled.

MCKENZIE WORE a knee-length blue cocktail dress with a flared skirt and cap sleeves. She was stunning, as always, and I was a very proud man to have her on my arm.

Ike had laid out our clothes again while we'd been lounging outside on our patio. Or Polly. Probably Polly, though I'm sure Ike had chosen the ensembles. Tonight, he'd decided to have mercy on McKenzie and picked out a pair of blue ballerina flats.

I hated to say it, but I was grateful to him.

The art at the gallery was by a new avant-garde artist who critics were raving about. I wasn't exactly impressed, but then dying bananas and rotting meat weren't really my thing.

"Please tell me you're not planning to buy any of this," McKenzie whispered to me as we walked around the gallery. Most people were holding flutes of champagne, but she and I had both declined. I think we were both off drinking for a long, long time.

"I don't know. The orange peel might look nice in our bedroom," I teased.

She made a face. "God no."

"Well, well, well. Fancy seeing you two here."

I took a deep breath and turned. It wasn't as though we hadn't been expecting Bran, but seeing him in the flesh made my blood boil.

McKenzie clung more tightly to my arm, and I wasn't sure if it was because she was trying to hold me back, because she was disturbed by him, or both.

"Bran," I said blandly. *Grandfather's taking care of this. I don't have to do anything but watch this asshole's life unravel,* I reminded myself, trying to stay calm.

"Will. Oh, McKenzie. You look lovely. Who did your make-up? I'll recommend them to Gwendolyn." He grinned.

It was secret option three that she was feeling. I suddenly had to grab her arms so she didn't attack him.

He laughed, even as several heads turned our way while she struggled to free herself from me.

"It won't be long now," I whispered in her ear. "Honeybee, let things unfold. Be patient."

"What won't be long now?" he asked, frowning at us, stopping mid-gloat.

Damn him and his sonar hearing! "We're leaving soon," I explained as she stopped struggling. I folded her back into my side.

"That's too bad. Is something the matter?" His smile was toxic, poisoning everyone and everything around him.

A woman in black holding a glass of champagne stopped me from answering by bumping between us. "Excuse me," she said. The look she gave me when she turned my way had me taking a cautious step backward, pulling McKenzie with me.

"You are not excused. We were having a conversa—" Bran began angrily.

Much like Sheila had at the charity benefit, the woman in black threw her champagne on him. Right in his face.

Only, it became immediately apparent that this was *not* champagne....

He screamed while the woman simply said, "Mr. Masterson sends his regards." Then she faded away as though she'd never been there to begin with.

Bran's face almost seemed to melt, an image I would never get out of my mind. I wasn't sure if that was a good thing or a bad thing. I tried shielding McKenzie from seeing the awful scene, but she pulled back.

"I want to watch," she stated.

I nodded and kept us rather close while others reacted and swarmed him, performing first aid. We simply watched while his outside changed to match what was inside.

Soon enough, Bran was carted away by ambulance.

"Oh dear. Must have been a jealous ex." Ike appeared out of nowhere, casually sipping a glass of champagne.

"Must have been," I agreed, my arm around McKenzie.

"Shame," she added.

"Yes. Terrible shame. One can only imagine the number of surgeries, painful ones, he will have to endure to restore his appearance. If it can ever be fully restored," he lamented.

I tried not to smirk. "That sounds awful."

"It will be," he promised darkly. "But he needed the reminder. A lasting one, as your grandfather said."

"Remind me to bring him his favorite cheesecake when we go visit," I replied.

Ike smiled. "He'll appreciate that. Speaking of which, he would like to see you this Saturday."

I nodded. "Seems only fair."

"Good. Visiting hours begin at one. I'll let him know you'll be there." He looked around the gallery and sighed. "What rubbish. I'll tell Polly to put your banana straight in the trash. We need to support the arts, after all."

"... Thank you, Ike," I said after a long pause.

"You're welcome, Will." He gave us both a wave, set his glass on the tray of a passing waiter, then headed out.

McKenzie looked up at me, troubled. "Is it a bad sign that I feel kind of good about what happened this evening?"

"No. It makes you human. Besides, then we'd both have to question our sanity," I responded, rubbing her arm. "I feel kind of good about it, too."

"But also a little horrified. And I have a whole new respect—or maybe fear—of your grandfather," she said, shuddering a bit.

I grimaced. "I was hoping you'd never find out about how scary he can really be. As long as we're never on the receiving end, I think we'll be okay."

"You knew this stuff about him before?" she asked, blinking at me.

"Not to this extent, no. But I've always known him to be a very determined man who always gets what he wants," I explained. "Right now, he wants us."

McKenzie swallowed. "That's scary, too."

FOUR
WHO AM I?

McKenzie

The car ride home was silent, mostly because of me. Officer Pence showed up at the gallery with Officer Edwards. I was beginning to think he was stalking us.

He glanced at Will and I once—just once—and I knew he knew. I knew he knew that we knew he knew. But instead of coming over to question us himself, he sent Officer Edwards.

Officer Edwards brought us to a corner of the gallery that smelled like hundred-year-old socks and just shrugged. "So. What's the official line?"

"Line?" I repeated.

"We were just here and some crazy lady showed up and threw acid on poor Bran," Will said without missing a beat. "We have no idea what could have motivated the attack."

It sounded genuine, like he'd rehearsed it in front of a mirror several times before we came. And maybe he had. If I'd known, I would have done the same. "Yeah, what he said."

"Uh-huh." He didn't believe us. I didn't blame him. "Then the fact he attacked Miss Kent last Saturday had absolutely nothing to do with it."

"Can't imagine how. We've been recuperating at home since then," Will said.

I leaned into his side, trying to absorb his confidence.

"These things can be hired out, you know," Officer Edwards pointed out.

Will's eyes widened. "Who would do such a thing?"

"Terrible, terrible thing," I added.

Officer Edwards snorted. "Fine. Detective Pence told me to get your statements for the record. I'm going to pretend like I believe you because I already know how this is going to go."

"Detective Pence?" I asked.

Officer Edwards nodded. "We both got promoted for a job well done. But mostly for keeping our mouths shut. You understand how these things work."

"We do," Will said. "And thank you for your hard work on this case. Hopefully, the woman is brought to justice."

"She'll be brought to the same justice Mr. Lockwood was brought to. Official justice, anyway." He sighed. "I don't even know why we're here."

"Keeping up appearances," Will replied.

"Exactly." Officer Edwards took a step back. "You two enjoy the rest of your evening. I'm sure you've got a lot to discuss."

Will hugged me closer to his side. "Thank you for all that you do, Officer."

"Doesn't feel like a whole lot these days," he muttered while making his way back over to *Detective* Pence.

"Hm." Will frowned after him.

"What?" I asked.

"It's just a shame. He and Detective Pence are good cops. If they've got our beat, they're going to be frustrated a lot," he said.

I was confused. "'Our beat'?"

"I like to call it the society beat. Where they'll be dealing with high society crimes for the most part," he explained.

"Oh." I gave it some thought. A lot of money was probably spent keeping a lot of crimes—minor *and* major—swept under the rug. "I can see where that would be frustrating."

Will rubbed my back. "How are you doing?"

"I... think I'd like to go home now." My emotions were such a riot of contradictions I couldn't nail one down to examine it before another bubbled up. It was exhausting.

"I like that idea." He guided me to the gallery door and out onto the sidewalk.

I wasn't even surprised to see our chauffeur already there, holding open the door to our sleek, black Mercedes.

Will helped me into the back seat then slid in beside me. He draped an arm across the back of my seat after we were buckled up, playing gently with my hair.

"Home?" the chauffeur asked.

"Yes, please, Rafael," Will said.

Rafael nodded and put the partition up once we were underway. I liked that he tried to give us the illusion of privacy, even though whatever was planted in the car were recording our every word.

"How are you feeling?" Will asked again.

I clenched and unclenched my fists in my lap. "I'm not sure."

"I kind of figured. I'm not sure how I'm feeling, either," he admitted.

Tears stung my eyes, and I leaned on his shoulder. "It was truly horrifying. I'm never going to forget it. But on the other hand, I feel like I needed to see it. Like now I can sleep better at night."

"I understand. Trust me." He kissed the top of my head. "I feel satisfied. Like justice has been served. Not an inch of me thinks it was too much or that he didn't deserve it. I'm trying to reconcile that with being a moral human being."

"Exactly!" I exclaimed. "That's exactly how I feel! I mean, what kind of person *am* I when I feel good about that kind of suffering?!

Bran's an asshole. No, he's a *monster*. But he also hurt Gwendolyn and could have killed you with the drugs he put in your tea—"

"Not to mention the small matter of beating you unconscious and trying to rape you," he reminded me.

I blushed. "Yes, well, it doesn't seem as important as you nearly getting killed. I mean, what would I do without you?" I shivered. "I think my whole soul would be ripped from my body."

He tilted my chin up and kissed me. "I love you, and you know I feel the same way. Which is why you're getting beaten half to death is not a small matter to me."

"True," I reluctantly admitted.

"I like the selflessness, but I for one, will never forgive him for what he did, and I hope he loses an eye," he said darkly.

"See? That's what I'm talking about! What kind of people are we when we're wishing that kind of misery on another person?!" I responded.

Will cupped my cheek. "Do you think I'm a monster for wishing him ill?"

"No! But...."

"I don't think you are, either. Like I said, we're human. And he's a very, very bad man. I'm glad we'll both sleep better knowing Grandfather has his eyes on Bran. There's not a lot I feel I can thank my grandfather for, but this? Yes," he said.

I chewed my lip. "I just feel like I'm not supposed to feel this... good. I felt relieved. I mean, I felt a lot of things watching that acid eat him up. But ultimately, I felt relieved. Like, closure."

"Me, too. I didn't feel as though I had this all-consuming anger anymore. I didn't have to carry it anymore because Grandfather took care of the situation—without having to drag either of us through court and the media's muckraking. I... just hated the idea of you being subjected to that after everything Bran already did. He would have insisted you asked for it—all that crap." He rubbed his hand over his face. "I know we're probably going to get burned by the media over this, that, and the other thing. It comes with the territory of being a kind of social celebrity. But that wasn't how I wanted us to start."

"What 'this, that, and the other thing'?" I asked, frowning. "Did we do something wrong? I mean, I know Bran would have been an absolute dickhead, but what else is there?"

"Well... I'm eleven years older than you." He winced.

I rolled my eyes. "Seriously? We're beating that dead horse again?"

"It's something they're going to latch onto. I don't think it'll become a big deal, considering men in their seventies in high society are still marrying twenty-year-olds, but they'll poke a little fun at it," he said.

"Let them. I know what I want. I know *who* I want. And I hope you do, too." I gave him a long look, our unspoken code for *we're leaving, anyway*.

He nodded. "I do know who I want. I can't imagine my life without you. That being said, I am going to find a way to propose properly without Ike's scheming and five hundred reporters watching. It'll probably be something small...."

"Thank God for that. I like small." I smiled at him. "If it's just the two of us sitting on the patio, I'd be completely happy. Over the moon, even. I might even go modern and propose to you first!"

"Don't you dare," he scolded me. "I only get one chance to do this right."

I gave him a soft kiss. "Okay. I was only kidding. Mostly."

"Yes, well, stick with the 'mostly' part." He stared off into the distance, idly playing with my hair.

"I don't want you to give yourself an ulcer trying to decide how to propose to me," I said.

Will smiled slightly. "It'd be a badge of honor. But no, I'm just trying to figure out how to get you an engagement ring without Ike's input. I know the monstrosity of a ring he's going to foist on us. It was my grandmother's. It's ugly as fuck."

I burst out laughing. "*That's* what you're worried about?!"

"You haven't seen this ring," he replied solemnly. "The best thing I can say about it is if we got lost at sea, we could use it as a boat anchor."

I laughed harder. "Oh my God, you're going to make me pee!"

He grinned. "Challenge accepted."

I swatted him. "Even if I had to wear the boat anchor, as long as it told the whole world I'm yours, that would be fine by me. Too bad men don't get engagement rings."

"Will a wedding ring do?" he asked softly.

My mouth went dry, and my heart pounded. I framed his face with my hands and kissed him thoroughly.

When we came up for air, I managed to gasp, "Yes. That will do nicely."

Will swallowed, his eyes burning with passion. "Rafael, I think you need to take the long way home."

"Very good, sir." The driver's voice came over the intercom.

Will undid his seatbelt then leaned over and did the same to mine, kissing my neck and collarbone hungrily.

I burned all over. It had been nearly a week since he'd touched me. I understood—I had a concussion, after all—but I still missed our physical connection desperately. We'd never gone so long without having sex.

"How are you feeling?" he asked against my skin, his hand massaging my breast through my cocktail dress.

"Needy," I answered, reaching down to open his fly. "How are you feeling?"

"Same. I just don't want to cause you too much strain...." He unzipped the back of my dress while he spoke.

I could have been half dead from the concussion and still wanted this. I knew I wasn't supposed to do anything really strenuous for at least a week. But the Masterson doctor had come to check on me daily and said I was healing well. "Will, if we don't make love this instant, my poor concussed brain is going to explode."

"Well, we can't have that." He drew me into his lap.

I finished freeing his dick from his pants and boxers. He was hard as a rock and leaked a little on my hand.

He groaned and pulled down my dress, exposing my breasts. I gasped as he began worrying my nipples with his teeth, first one, then the other.

I stroked his shaft. "Will?"

"Yesss?" he managed, bringing his head up from feasting on my breasts.

"I'm still wearing underwear." I pouted.

His lips parted, and he licked them slowly, sending a thrill of desire through me. "I can fix that."

"Good." I widened my thighs, knowing what he was about to do.

Will pushed my skirt up and snapped my panties right off. Then he took my hips and guided me down onto his cock.

I moaned as he pushed up into me, filling me to the brim. It seemed like the length of him would never end!

"That's it, honeybee. Take it all. It's been a while, but I know you still can," he whispered hotly in my ear as he rubbed my clit while giving me the last two inches of him.

I had to take several deep breaths. I gripped his shirt and buried my face in his neck.

He danced his fingers up and down my bare back, not moving, letting me get used to him again. He was a lot to handle, even when we were going at it regularly.

Now, I felt like I was climbing Mt. Everest without oxygen.

Will kissed my temple. "You okay?"

I nodded. "Just need... a minute... damn... keep forgetting... how big you are!"

He chuckled. "You always give the best compliments."

I squeezed my inner muscles, and he groaned. "Don't make fun."

"Okay. Lesson learned." He touched me everywhere, light, loving little touches.

Soon enough, I was ready. "Sit still," I told him. Then I started to ride him.

Will threw his head back against the seat, his hands on my hips, trying to 'help.'

I pulled his hands off my hips. "No, no. You've been bad. You're going to have to sit there and let me screw your brains out. No touching."

"What?!" His voice was strained. "Honeybee, I said I learned my lesson."

I gave him an impish smile. "I don't think you've learned it well enough."

FIVE

LESSON LEARNED

Will

I tried to grab her hips again, but she smacked my hands.

"Oh no you don't. You're going to lay back and enjoy it like a good boy," McKenzie said.

That phrase alone was enough to make my cock twitch with need. "Honeybee…" I wheedled.

She shook her head and put a finger over my lips. "No whining."

"I'm not—!" I protested. But it ended in a groan when she started moving up and down on me.

"Good boy," she said, a light sweat breaking out over her body as she rode me.

She glistened, and I wanted to lick every inch of her. Especially her large, full, delectable breasts that kept bouncing in my face when she reached the top of my cock.

My tongue darted out of its own accord, catching a nipple, and she gasped. "Will!"

"Yes?" I replied innocently.

She sat down on my dick and squeezed her inner muscles.

I yelped, almost cumming right then and there. "Honeybee!"

"Yes?" she said just as innocently.

"Okay. Okay, I've been a very naughty boy. Please—*please*—let me fuck you properly," I begged.

McKenzie pretended to think about it, tapping her chin. "Well... I suppose...."

It was all the permission I needed. I rolled her underneath me on the seat while she squealed, grabbed her ass with one hand, a breast with the other, and began to have my wicked way with her.

"Will!" she exclaimed, holding on for dear life.

"Just sit back and enjoy it," I teased, licking her glistening skin.

She giggled then gasped as I thrust hard, fast, and deep. "You're... going to make me so sore...."

I paused deep inside her. "Is that okay?"

McKenzie scratched my shoulders. "I didn't say you should stop!"

With a chuckle, I began thrusting again. "The lovemaking department won't be taking any more complaints today. We're out at the job site."

"Good. Now work hard," she panted, clinging to me as her body rocked with my thrusts.

"Always do," I responded. I squeezed her ass again then moved my hand down from her breast and worked it between us so I could play with her clit.

She arched into me, clamping down on my cock as she came, her nails dragging down my skin. "Will!!!"

I groaned and rammed in hard, as deep as I could possibly go, and erupted inside her, a week of pent up need filling her up. I'd never been so grateful for an IUD in all my life because I could never have worn a condom with her. I needed to feel her, just like this.

Come to think of it, she was the only woman I'd ever had bare. The thought surprised me as I held her in the aftermath, both of us panting as we came down. No matter what a woman had ever told me, I'd always worn a condom. Always.

"What?" she asked, running her fingers through my hair, our bodies still intimately joined.

"Nothing I want to talk about. Just a passing thought," I said, kissing her to distract her. My cock wouldn't have minded another round, and I turned the kiss white hot to let her know that.

McKenzie was not derailed. "Will!" she laughed, pulling back a little so I had to settle for feasting on her neck. "Yes, okay! I'd like to go again, too. But first, I want to know what that weird look on your face was for!"

"But if I tell you, we might not go again," I replied, trying not to whine. I never imagined myself as a man who whined, and begged, and had sex in the back of the car knowing full well Ike, and Rafael, and God only knew who else was listening. If I had to choose between that and never touching McKenzie again, however... well, it wasn't really a choice.

"Now you have to tell me," she insisted.

I sighed. "I was just thinking about how we've never used a condom, that's all."

She looked confused. "Right... but I have an IUD. It lasts five years."

"I know. I know. That's not the... um...." I rubbed the back of my neck. "I don't like talking about other women with you."

McKenzie blinked, still confused. Then realization dawned. "You've always worn a condom with the others."

"I wouldn't call them 'others.' That suggests they somehow compare to you," I said. "And I wasn't thinking about other women while we were making love. I was thinking about protection after."

"The IUD should be really effective, but if you think we should start using condoms..." she began.

I made a face. "No. I'd really rather not."

She frowned. "Then I don't understand."

"It's just... I always used them because, no matter what they said out loud, I knew any one of them would happily try to baby trap me. Lie to me. But I've never once doubted a word you've said. And honestly? I'd like to have kids with you. I mean, not *now*. You're nineteen, and there's still a lot you want to do with your life before that. Anyway, it was just a passing thought," I muttered.

McKenzie then shocked me by smiling at me. She looped her arms around my neck. "You're so sweet."

"Not... the answer I was expecting, but tell me more," I said, stroking her arm.

"You just said you trust me and want to build a life with me. Sure, it might not have come out exactly like that, but that's what you meant." She fused her lips to mine in a searing kiss.

I groaned. "Please tell me this means I get to get lucky again."

She laughed. "One track mind. But yes, you get to get lucky again."

Score!

In truth, between two more rounds in the back of the car and another three in bed when we got home, we probably strained the powers of her IUD to the breaking point. When we did finally pass out in each other's arms, I slept better than I had in years.

It was in the twilight hours when I felt her hand stroke across my chest and a soft kiss on my shoulder. "I love you," she whispered.

I smiled and threaded my fingers through hers. "I love you, too."

MCKENZIE WASN'T there when I woke up.

I sat up, wondering how I could have slept through her leaving the bed. It seemed impossible! I jumped out and threw on some boxers before going to find her, trying not to listen to the panic in my chest.

She was out on the patio with the doctor. I could have died from the relief I felt. "McKenzie, don't scare me like that," I said, sitting next to her, completely ignoring the doctor's presence.

With a frown, she tugged on the leg of my boxers. "You didn't want to get dressed?" She was wearing a T-shirt and shorts. Normal.

Casual. Comfortable. Nothing to suggest we needed to go anywhere or do anything today.

I liked that.

"I was afraid something had happened to you," I admitted, leaning my head on her shoulder. "I wanted to get to you as fast as I could."

McKenzie winced and wrapped an arm around me. "I'm sorry. I should have woken you up. I will next time. You know, after all we've been through, I probably would have freaked out, too."

"Exactly." I looked at the doctor. "How's she doing?"

The doctor took that as permission to unload on me. "When I said 'light exercise,' I didn't mean six rounds of sex in the span of an evening."

I glanced at her. "You told him?" I mouthed.

"I can still hear you," the doctor grumped.

She shrugged sheepishly. "He asked. And he's my doctor. I figured I was supposed to tell him."

"That she was!" He interrupted anything I would have said. "She's still concussed. I will order another CT scan. You will need to bring McKenzie back to the hospital to have it done. I imagine they will be able to get you in later today, but I will call you to let you know when." He snapped his very cliché doctor's bag closed.

"But... doesn't that usually take a while? Aren't there people waiting with appointments?" she asked.

The doctor looked at her and just sighed then turned back to me. "Once I have the results of the scan, *then* we can discuss further bedroom activities."

"Yes, sir," I said, sounding contrite but really not regretting a moment.

"Good. All right, I'll be in touch. I'm assuming I'll be speaking with Polly first?" he asked.

That got under my skin. Not that it was the doctor's fault, but McKenzie and I still hadn't been allowed cell phones. "Yes, I believe you will be speaking with Polly. She'll relay the message."

"I suppose that works. I'm a little insulted you keep fobbing me off on your staff when it's regarding your own health, but if that's what you prefer..." he sniffed.

"It's not what we prefer," I replied, grinding my teeth. "We just don't currently have phones."

He appeared taken aback. "You don't have phones?"

"We're trying a technology-free cleanse," McKenzie said quickly, elbowing me.

"Sure are," I grunted.

The doctor rolled his eyes. "Honestly, all these new-age fixes. You should really consult a doctor before doing crazy things. Well, I don't suppose it can hurt. I'll see you tomorrow." He took his bag and left.

"We're playing nice," she reminded me, elbowing me again.

I grimaced. "Yes, fine, okay."

She laughed and gave me a kiss. "Someone woke up on the wrong side of the bed."

"I can't help it. My body pillow ran away." I smiled.

McKenzie kissed me. "So, I was looking at the pool, and I saw you have this nice little hidden grotto at one end under a waterfall...."

"God no!" I all but shouted.

Her eyebrows drew together with hurt. "You don't want to do it? Is it because of what the doctor said?"

"I want to do it," I assured her. "Hell, I *always* want to do it with you. We could be in a pit of nails and razor blades, and I'd *still* want to do it. But... I once saw footage of your parents while they were here. They were under surveillance, too...."

She wrinkled her nose. "Are you trying to tell me my parents had sex in the grotto?"

I swallowed. "Yes."

McKenzie burst into giggles. "Will, you'd have to know my parents, but they are very much in love, even to this day, and I've caught them just about everywhere."

"R-Really?" I asked.

"Absolutely. Hayloft. Living room. Tractor...." She ticked the locations off on her fingers. "In a place like this? I doubt there are many options left open to us that they didn't have sex in before."

"You... had a most interesting childhood." I thought of her having the loving parents she had. Parents who genuinely loved each other. I tried not to be envious.

She stopped laughing. "Oh, Will." She climbed into my lap and stroked my cheek. "We both know my parents wanted you. If your grandfather hadn't gotten in the way, you would have had a most interesting childhood, too. Warm, and loving, and full of laughter."

I kissed her palm. "If that had happened, though, I might have thought of you more like a sister, and that would have been tragic. To have you? I'd do it all again."

Her eyes shimmered with tears and she kissed me. "I still don't like your grandfather."

"I don't either," I agreed.

"Even if he did punish Bran," she added.

"I know," I said.

She bit her lip. "We're really seeing him tomorrow?"

"We are."

"Well, I hope Ike picks something with flats," she sighed.

"From your lips to the recording devices' ears." I smirked.

McKenzie swatted me. "You know there are now recordings of *us* having sex."

I made a face. "I know. I'm sorry."

"It's not your fault. I'm just saying maybe we should re-christen the grotto," she teased.

I groaned and tickled her. "You'll have to do a lot to convince me."

She shrieked with laughter then wiggled in my lap so she was straddling me and gave me a kiss that shook me to my toes.

"Okay. I'm convinced," I murmured.

SIX
THE MAN HIMSELF

McKenzie

Ike chose a cute yellow sundress with daisies on it for me. It appeared after Will and I got back from our third foray into the grotto Saturday morning. After my CT scan, the doctor had reluctantly admitted that my concussion had improved a lot, though he had still been adamant about not overexerting myself.

Will took this to mean we could only have sex three times a day. I didn't correct him. I liked that interpretation, too.

Now, however, we were doing the unavoidable. We were going to see the man himself—William Masterson Sr.

"He picked out some flats," Will pointed out while I sat nervously next to him in the back of the Mercedes, being driven once again by Rafael.

I knew he was trying to put me at ease, but I was practically trembling. With rage or fear, I wasn't sure. Probably both. "Yes, Ike is a real gem."

He snorted. "We'll have to agree to disagree on that one. I'm just hanging on to how grateful I am for them taking care of Bran. I figure it might get me through at least an hour sitting face-to-face with Grandfather after everything that's happened."

"No shouting. We're playing nice," I reminded him, though I was the one who might end up shouting, and I was sure he knew it.

Will squeezed my hand. "No shouting," he agreed. "Neither one of us is going to start screaming at him."

"I'm going to have 'play nice' going on repeat in my head the entire time we're there," I said. "I'm hoping it'll help."

"Me, too." He kissed my hand, and then the car stopped.

We'd been driving for an hour. But, as we sat outside the Faribault, Minnesota, prison, I realized that hadn't been nearly long enough to prepare. A year probably wouldn't have been long enough.

"Breathe," Will whispered while Rafael opened my door.

I scooted out of the car while Will opened his own door and came around to the other side so he could take my hand. I tried to concentrate on my breathing, but I was more nervous than I'd ever been in my life.

"The car will be ready when your visit ends," Rafael said with great professionalism.

"Er... thanks," I replied.

"We'll only be an hour. That's the limit," Will told him.

"Very good, sir." Rafael got back in the car.

I gulped as Will led me into the facility. We passed through security then were shown to the visiting room.

Masterson was already there, sitting, waiting. He smiled as we approached.

I wanted to slap him. "Playing nice. Playing nice," I murmured under my breath.

Will squeezed my hand before settling me in a chair across from his grandfather. Then he sat down next to me. "Grandfather."

"Will. It's so good to see you. It's been a while," Masterson said with a smile.

That smile was positively chilling, even though I'm sure it was meant to put us at ease. I tried to remind myself this older, gray-haired grandfather was just a man. Just a man.

But he exuded power like it was a strong cologne, and considering everything he'd done, that scared the shit out of me.

"I wanted to thank you for clearing up that situation we had," Will said, noting my stiffness and squeezing my hand under the table. "It was... the perfect solution."

"I'm nothing if not good at balancing the books." He turned to me. "McKenzie, you look lovely. You've grown into a fine young woman. I still remember when you were rolling around in the barnyard mud, throwing handfuls of the stuff at your parents. They were *quite* indulgent, but then, it's in their nature."

I stared at him, my jaw on the floor. "How...?"

"Grandfather, please be nice." Will frowned at Masterson. "I'm sure you have plenty of footage somewhere of McKenzie growing up. You don't have to scare her."

"I might. I might not." He winked. "The walls have ears here, you know."

"I know the feeling." Will sounded pissed.

"Playing nice," I whispered, recovering myself.

Will took a deep breath. "You wanted to see us?"

Masterson looked smug. "I did. I just wanted to congratulate you on your upcoming engagement and nuptials. I should be out by the time the wedding happens, but, sadly, will likely miss the engagement party. Unfortunately, Bran will no longer be able to host, but I'm working on other ideas. It seems he had an accident."

"Terribly unfortunate," Will replied with a flat affect.

"Oh yes, that's right. You were there. It must have been awful to witness." Masterson clucked his tongue.

"Truly awful," Will said with the same affect.

Masterson chuckled. "How about you, McKenzie? What did you think?"

"I thought it was... well, whoever was behind it was very thorough. They still haven't found the woman in black," I responded.

"It's good to be thorough." Masterson sat back in his chair with a self-satisfied smirk. "I'll have to have Ike send him some flowers."

"He'll probably appreciate that," Will said.

"There are a lot of things Bran needs to learn to appreciate. But now he has all the time in the world to reflect on himself," Masterson replied. "Now then. Will, you will be returning to the office on Monday and learning more of the ropes from Ike. No more languishing at your desk, waiting for the next party to attend."

Will nodded, though he wasn't happy about it. "I figured I'd be going back soon."

"Good instincts. McKenzie, I've heard you want to finish school. That's an excellent ambition. Have you decided which school you'd like to attend? And a major?" Masterson asked.

"I... was going to the U of M..." I said, wondering why he was asking me about schools.

"I know. I just thought you might want to go somewhere a little more ambitious. It's a fine school, don't get me wrong. I was just thinking, now that you're with Will, Carleton College might be a better fit. Of course, I'd prefer to send you to Harvard, Stanford, or some such, but Carleton is a decent school with a good Political Science and International Relations program. You could become a great asset to Will." Masterson gestured to his grandson. "Will was a passably good student at Yale—a Master's in Business, of course. But he didn't really have the drive for it. You strike me as a young lady with a lot of fire. I think you would be excellent in a program like that."

"Why can't she go to Harvard or Stanford?" Will cut in.

Masterson chuckled. "Because of you, my dear boy. What are you going to do while she's off on one of the coasts? You'll sit here pining your heart out, and you will be absolutely *useless* to the company."

"I'd be useless without you, too," I whispered when Will scowled, unable to argue the point.

"Of course you would," Masterson said, having heard me anyway. "Now, I know your credits from last year will transfer. All of them. And you won't be penalized for missing this semester. I have made sure of it."

"So, basically I'm going to Carleton College," I replied, my stomach twisting at how this man already had my future all laid out for me.

"Yes," he confirmed. "After you've finished your degree, we'll talk about you continuing at Harvard for an advanced degree. You'd be invaluable as an International Trade Specialist. Of course, you will also need to learn a few languages. Chinese will be a must and Spanish. I'll consult with Ike to see if there are any others that will be absolutely critical to your role."

"My role?" I echoed faintly.

Masterson shrugged. "You can decline, of course. You just don't strike me as the kind of person who likes languishing at home, waiting for her man to show up every night."

He wasn't wrong there. *Playing nice.* Besides, it could be a nice way to pass the time until Will and I escaped.

"Okay," I said. "I'll do it."

Will looked startled. "McKenzie, you really don't have to."

"No, I want to. If I'm being offered a top-notch education instead of wandering around an empty house every day, I'm going to take it," I told him.

"Smart girl." Masterson was very pleased with himself. "This has been a most productive meeting. I look forward to seeing you next Saturday."

"Next Saturday?" Will repeated.

Masterson nodded. "Of course. Every Saturday until I leave this hellhole. Then, I'll be home, and back in the office. We'll have family dinners, it will be lovely."

Will had gone pale, and I was sure I was the same. I felt the blood completely drain from my face.

Masterson laughed loudly. "You'll get used to it. Pretty soon, we'll be one big happy family."

"Grandfather... with respect..." Will began.

"Playing nice," I mumbled, though my guts were twisted with horror.

"Yes, Will. Let's remember to play nice," Masterson said. "I know it doesn't seem like it now, but this is going to work. We're going to *make* it work." He shook his head sadly. "It could have gone so well with Jacey, Caleb, and your father. People are usually just too stubborn for their own good."

Will's father? I glanced at him, worried. What would he think of his grandfather bringing Will Jr. up this way? So... casually?

I was right to be concerned. Will was shaking. "You sonofa—"

Grabbing Will's arm, I stood, tugging him up after me. "It's been so nice to see you, Mr. Masterson. I'm looking forward to next Saturday."

"I'm sure you are." Masterson grinned.

I began pulling Will away from the table. At first, he wouldn't budge, glaring at his grandfather. If looks could kill, Masterson would have been a steaming pile of ash.

"Will," I whispered. "Let's go home."

He stood still, immovable, for another minute, then turned his back on his grandfather. "See you Saturday," he bit out.

"Oh, and McKenzie?" Masterson called sweetly after us.

Dread sank like a stone from my throat to my stomach. "Yes, sir?"

"I'm sorry about your parents," he said, his voice dripping with false sympathy.

"Yes, well, we all make mistakes," I replied sweetly. "Will, let's go."

Will stopped me. "Grandfather, what have you done?"

Masterson's eyes widened innocently. "Me? No. They still don't know who it was. They're still figuring out the wreckage."

"Wreckage?" I asked. "I don't understand what you're talking about."

"That's right. You haven't been watching much television. Busy, busy, busy," Masterson said.

"Grandfather." Will pulled me back to the table and leaned over it. "What have you *done*?!"

Masterson shrugged. "Nothing, of course. Nothing at all." But his eyes danced with mirth. "Someone blew up an FBI safe house in Oakdale, however. They haven't sorted everything out yet, but...."

My heart seized. Will grabbed me just as I was going to leap across the table and throttle the old sonofabitch.

"Where are my parents?!" I screamed.

Will's arms banded around me like iron, and he put a hand over my mouth. "Shh. He's just playing with you. Don't let him."

This was rich coming from the guy who'd nearly decked Masterson for talking smack about his father. But, as a guard walked over, I understood that now was not the time or place.

Besides, like Will said, Masterson would only play with me some more. We'd have to get our information from a more reliable source.

"What's going on over here?" the guard asked gruffly, hands on hips.

"We just received some bad news, that's all," Will replied, rubbing my shoulders.

"Yeah, well, keep it down," he said.

Will nodded. "Sorry. We were just leaving, anyway."

"I'll have him put back in his cell." He motioned to some other guards.

"Good," Will said with a touch of darkness.

I felt the same way.

When we got back to the car, I turned to Will, but he'd already knocked on the partition. "Rafael," he said, "call Ike, then give me your phone."

"Sir, I think Mr. Freeborn is busy—" Rafael protested.

Will slapped the transom between us. "I'm not asking, Rafael!"

He swallowed and pressed a contact on the phone mounted to

the dashboard. Then he took it out of its dock and handed it back to Will.

"Rafael? What's the problem?" I heard Ike's clipped tone even as Will put the phone to his ear.

"Where are the Killeens?" Will demanded.

SEVEN
INFERNO

Will

I waited, not quite so patiently, for Ike to collect himself. "Well?!"

"Will, it's always good to hear from you," he recovered smoothly. "I'm surprised you managed to get a hold of Rafael's phone."

"He gave it to me. I was very convincing. Now shut the fuck up and tell me what happened to McKenzie's parents," I snapped.

"Well, Will, how am I supposed to 'shut the fuck up' and tell you what happened to the Killeens at the same time?" Ike asked, laughing.

The sonofabitch actually laughed!

"Ike, I swear to Jesus..." I growled.

"Put me on speaker. I think McKenzie should hear it from the horse's mouth, so to speak," he replied.

I wasn't so sure about that. Whatever it was, it was bad news, and he had all the delicacy of a hammer. "You can tell me."

"Speaker, Will. I don't want to repeat myself," he insisted.

Grinding my teeth, I pulled the phone away from my ear and pressed the speaker icon. "You're on speaker," I grumbled.

"Excellent. Now, from what I've seen on the news, it seems someone bombed an FBI safe house in Oakdale. Terrible tragedy," he said.

"Why tragic? Was there someone in there?" I hazarded a guess.

"Oh, a few agents. The explosion also got the car outside with Attorney General Joy Packard in it. And another agent. There was quite a bit of blood and bits, but the impression is that there were two high-profile witnesses in the back who... may or may not have survived. Caleb and Jocelyn Kent, also known as Killeen," Ike said. "Of course, the top story is the death of Ms. Packard, so it's been difficult to get much else. It would be nice if the Killeens had been stopped on a more permanent basis, however. Then your grandfather could come home without delay."

McKenzie lost all color. I wrapped my arm around her, pulling her into my chest. "What makes you think the Killeens might have been... permanently stopped?"

"Their blood is at the scene. Quite a bit of it. Not a fatal amount, but then...." I could almost hear him shrug.

"He can stop now," McKenzie whispered.

"You can stop now, Ike. Thank you for taking my call," I said and hung up before he could protest. I handed the phone back through the partition to Rafael then put both arms around her. "He said they haven't found any evidence of them being dead, just injured. And, knowing your parents, they probably got away. Grandfather would agree that they're very hard to keep down."

She hiccuped, and I could tell she was trying not to cry. "That's true."

I unlocked my seatbelt and hers and pulled her into my lap. "It's okay, honeybee. You can cry. This is very disturbing news."

McKenzie trembled, still fighting it, then burst into tears, wrapping her arms around my neck.

I rocked her and kissed her shoulder. "They'll show up. I mean, maybe not on our doorstep, but they're going to turn up somewhere. I know it."

"Why does this keep happening to our family, Will? What did my parents do wrong?!" she cried.

"As I understand it, they went out of bounds on a camping trip," I sighed. "When your mother was about your age."

"That's so stupid!" She shook her head, her chin rubbing against my shoulder. "So stupid."

"It really is," I agreed.

She sat up a bit, looking stricken. "I can't believe they never told me we were in such danger."

"I don't think they thought you were anymore." I lowered my eyes. "I keep thinking, if I hadn't shown up on your doorstep, none of this would have happened."

McKenzie shook her head. "No. Masterson would have shot a missile at the farm or something. He always knew we were there. Remember when he talked about me playing in the mud? That really happened."

I thought of arguing that it was still my fault, but then, she was right about the missile. As his court date got closer, it would not have surprised me at all if he'd done something like that.

"You might have saved us, Will," she said softly.

"I... hope so. And I mean it about your parents. They're scrappy," I responded.

She laughed through her tears. "'Scrappy'?"

"Well, they are." I blushed. "Is 'scrappy' an old man word or something?"

"You're not an old man." She poked me in the chest. "So, I guess we just... wait for a sign?"

Rafael cleared his throat. "There's been a sign."

"What?!" we shouted together.

He took his earbud out and put the sound on whatever he was listening to.

"... Witnesses Caleb and Jocelyn Killeen have been brought to Fairview Woodwinds Hospital in Woodbury, having escaped a bombing in Oakdale. Their conditions have not been made public.

Witnesses to the scene have stated that Mr. and Mrs. Killeen were able to walk several blocks before collapsing beside the road. An ambulance was called, and the two are now receiving medical care. It is unclear what they know about the death of Attorney General Joy Packard or if they were involved—"

"Involved?!" McKenzie's eyes widened. "*Involved?!*"

"These people just want ratings," I soothed. "At least now we know where they are. Rafael, we're going to Woodbury. And I swear to God, if you don't take us there, we'll do a tuck and roll out of this car and walk."

Rafael swallowed and locked the doors. "I will have to clear your request with Mr. Freeborn, sir."

"Then clear it with Mr. Freeborn," I ordered.

"Very good, sir." He turned off the news and made a call to Ike. "Mr. Freeborn...."

"Take them," Ike said without hesitation.

"Yes, sir. At once." Rafael took a different exit than what we'd taken to get to the prison.

I held McKenzie as he drove, counting down the seconds. It was a long, silent ride, but soon enough, Rafael was dropping us off at the front door of the hospital.

There was a crowd of reporters, but men in dark suits stationed at the door were not letting them in.

I walked with McKenzie straight up to one of the men in a black suit. "I'm William Masterson the Third."

The agent looked bored. "And?"

"Try putting that over your com," I said. I looked over at McKenzie. "This is McKenzie—"

"Killeen," McKenzie finished.

The agent blinked then spoke to someone on the other end of his com. The response he got made his eyebrows shoot straight up. "This way, please."

We got a two-person escort through the lobby and into the elevators. We passed a nurses' station and went straight to a room, the door of which was being guarded by another two agents. One of them held the door open.

McKenzie burst into the room. "Mom? Dad?"

I followed after her, hoping the Killeens were okay.

Jacey was sitting up in bed, poking at a food tray. Her arm was bandaged, but she didn't seem that much worse for the wear. "McKenzie!" she cried, shoving her tray away and opening her arms.

She went straight to her mother, carefully wrapping her in a hug. "Are you okay? Are you hurt? Where's Dad?"

One of the agents helpfully pushed back the curtain that separated the beds of the double room. Caleb was lying on his stomach and his back was covered in bandages. He was asleep.

"Dad!" McKenzie looked over at her father, her face pale with concern.

"It's all right, honey. He was awake not long ago. He's just resting up now. Of course your stubborn father had to go and save my life," Jacey sighed.

McKenzie snorted a laugh. "Of course. He wouldn't be Dad otherwise."

"Mrs. Killeen, I'm so very sorry," I finally interrupted, shuffling forward.

"Oh, Will. There will never be anything you need to be sorry for." Jacey let McKenzie go over to see her father and reached out to me.

I went to her, not sure what she wanted. Then I was wrapped in the strongest, most loving hug I'd ever had in my life.

"You're a good boy. I'm just sorry we couldn't keep you," Jacey said tearfully. "I want you to know you were wanted. So wanted."

I had the strongest urge to cry. I cleared my throat. "Thank you, Mrs. Killeen."

"Call me Jacey. Or maybe Mom. I hear you're planning to marry McKenzie, so it's only fitting," she replied.

If I call her Mom, I really am going to cry. "I am planning to marry McKenzie. I've never wanted anything more."

"I'm glad. I mean, it's an unusual relationship, but who am I to talk?" She laughed, releasing me.

I smiled. "I guess you could say that. Unusual or not, I'm never letting her go."

"Good. Of course, Caleb will want you to ask for formal permission," she warned me.

I squared my shoulders. "I absolutely will."

"And we'll want to be at the wedding, no matter how this all shakes out," she continued.

"We'd both want you there, even if it ends up being a little courthouse ceremony. You know, however this all shakes out," I said.

"And—"

Caleb groaned. "What's all the talking?" he asked, turning his head our way. He glanced up. "McKenzie!"

"Daddy!" she sobbed. I could tell she was trying to figure out how to hug him, but had to settle for putting a hand on a small bare patch on his arm. "I've been so worried! How are you feeling? Does it hurt really bad?"

"I've been better," he chuckled. "But we've been in worse spots than this." He looked over at me. "Will?"

"Mr. Killeen," I responded.

"You're sleeping with my daughter. I think we might be on a first name basis now," he said.

McKenzie blushed, and I frowned. "I don't appreciate your tone."

"Caleb! Be nice," Jacey scolded him.

He tried to shrug and winced. "I'm just saying."

"There are some things you keep in your head and don't say out loud. Honestly," Jacey sighed.

"Caleb, are you all right?" I asked.

"What doesn't kill you makes you stronger, right?" he joked.

McKenzie made a distressed sound.

"Really, I'm fine, my darling," he said, giving her a smile.

"He'll be fine. You know your father," Jacey said, though I could tell it was a little strained.

"Remember that time I stepped on the pitchfork? I recovered just fine," he reassured McKenzie.

"Dad, this is a lot more than a pitchfork," she replied worriedly.

I walked over and put an arm around her. "Your father will have the best doctors. Don't worry."

Caleb's eyes narrowed on me. "You make it sound like I'm going to accept help from Masterson."

"Look, you might have a grudge against my grandfather, which I understand. I do, too. But I don't mind spending his money to help you," I said. "You can stay with us until you're well enough to take off again. Hell, take us with you! You're a lot better at this disappearing thing than I am, clearly.'

"Will... the last time we were in Masterson's house... your father killed himself to try to get us out. And even that didn't work," he told me, dropping his whole attitude. In fact, he sounded sad and wracked with guilt.

I swallowed. "Oh."

"We can just go with the FBI. You should, too," Jacey said quickly. "I mean, you're already here."

"Ike would never have let us come here if he thought for a second he couldn't force us to go back home," I responded, a knot forming in my throat. It was good to hear my father hadn't just given in and offed himself, not that I wouldn't have understood. He'd actually done something heroic. Or tried to, at least.

With a grimace, Caleb reached out and patted my knee. "Masterson is not all-powerful."

"I'll let him know you said that."

I whirled around.

There stood Ike in the doorway, grinning from ear to ear.

EIGHT
BACK IN HELL

McKenzie

I didn't know what else to do. I stood in front of my father's bed, arms wide, putting myself between Ike and him.

Will did the same, only he moved to the other side of Mom's bed to stand in front of all of us. "What do you want?" he growled.

Ike laughed. "My aren't we prickly. Don't panic. I'm not here to hurt anyone."

"As opposed to blowing up the safe house?" Dad said pointedly.

"That was a terrible tragedy," Ike lamented. "You never know what people will do nowadays. Or how far they'll go to get what they want."

"Which brings me back to, what do you want, Ike? Or rather, what does *he* want?" Will asked.

Ike shrugged. "His freedom, of course. I'm here with a proposal. Caleb, you and Jacey will return to the Masterson Estate to recuperate and kindly decline any more silly requests to testify. You won't get into trouble. In fact, I think we'd have an excellent case against the government for being so poorly equipped to keep you safe. On multiple occasions. You should really sue. I can help."

"You can't be serious." Dad scoffed. "I know once we get back into the estate there's no getting out. We'll be there forever."

"In the lap of luxury, with your daughter," Ike said. "Not a bad trade-off."

"I have a counter offer," Dad replied. "Will, McKenzie, Jacey, and I all disappear. You never see or hear from us again. We don't fucking testify, and you leave us the *fuck* alone!"

I noticed the strain it was putting on Dad's body to shout at Ike. I touched his arm in the one spot that wasn't bandaged. "Dad, you need to calm down," I whispered.

"I'll calm down when this fucker is gone," he said, glaring at me then at Ike. "That's a take-it-or-leave-it offer."

"Then I'm afraid I'm going to have to leave it. Mr. Masterson has big plans for Will." Ike examined his nails. "Though, perhaps, I could convince Mr. Masterson to let the three of you go... in exchange for not testifying. Naturally, we would be keeping an eye on you at all times. But then, we always have. Surely you've realized that by now."

I snorted. There was no way I was going anywhere without Will.

"Yes. I have realized that." Dad looked up at me. "You'd let the three of us go?"

What?! I couldn't believe my father was even considering it! "Dad...."

"They accept," Will said.

WHAT?!!! "They most certainly do not!" I yelled.

Ike laughed. "Now there's going to be trouble in paradise. Why don't we start with bringing you back to the estate and getting you both healthy? Then we can discuss the details of your freedom."

"We're not falling for that trick," Dad said. "Once he has us, we're at his mercy."

"Hm. True. Unfortunately, you don't have a choice." Ike made a motion.

It was only then that I saw his bodyguard outside the door with a gurney.

"What the hell do you think you're doing, Ike?!" Will snapped as Ike's bodyguard wheeled the gurney inside, accompanied by two men in scrubs.

"My job. Stand aside, Will." Ike waved a hand as though swatting a fly.

Will stood firm. "Hey, FBI! I'd like to report a kidnapping in progress! *HELLO!!!*"

Ike rolled his eyes. "Your constant faith in the goodness of mankind is quaint."

No one came.

"Hey!" Will tried again, getting between the gurney and Dad's bed.

"Horacio." Ike sounded bored.

The bodyguard moved the gurney aside and went after Will.

"Stop!" I grabbed Horacio's arm as the two of them grappled. Will was strong, but Horacio had clearly trained with the marines or something because he knew the moves to subdue him.

"McKenzie, I really wouldn't get involved," Ike warned me.

I didn't let go. "Help! Help us!"

Two FBI agents came in.

Relief washed over me. "Masterson's goons are trying to kidnap my parents! You have to stop them!"

Will was struggling in Horacio's grasp, making loud sounds of frustration.

Horacio got tired of me hanging on him and finally threw me aside. I crashed into one of Dad's monitors.

The FBI agents did nothing.

"Help us!" I said again.

The agents glanced at me briefly then went over to Horacio, who was having a hard time with Will. I wanted to cheer my man on. But I wasn't sure what was happening.

One of them took out a syringe.

"Hey! Hey, stop! What do you think you're doing!" I screamed, stepping forward. My head throbbed.

I turned and realized I'd broken the screen on the monitor. I put a hand to my head and it came back bloody.

"McKenzie!" Mom cried.

"McK—!" Will started then sagged in Horacio's arms.

The FBI agent pulled the now empty syringe back. "These people are a real pain in the ass."

"Tell me about it," Ike grumped. "The doctor and his team are already set up at the estate. I suppose he'll have to look at you, too, now."

"What the hell is happening here?!" I asked, desperately looking around.

"The inevitable, McKenzie. Now, sit down by your mother and stop making this difficult. We want to make this as painless as possible for your father," Ike said.

Horacio dumped Will next to my mother on her bed.

At the same time, the FBI agents secured the gurney next to Dad's bed and began lifting him carefully from one to the other.

I took the opportunity to push past Ike and run to the door. "Help!" I yelled, running to the nurses' station. "Help, call security! Call somebody!"

The nurses at the station looked away, pretending I wasn't there.

I saw a security guard, but he also wouldn't look at me.

A doctor came walking down the hall, and I ran to him, grabbing him by the front of his white coat. "Help! They're trying to take my dad away, and he's not in any condition to leave!"

The doctor peeled my hands away. "He'll be fine."

"He'll be—what kind of doctor *are* you?!" I shouted in his face.

"One with student loans," he replied. Then he pushed me away from him, turned on his heel, and walked away.

A hand fell on my shoulder, and I whipped around, coming face-to-face with Ike.

"McKenzie, are you finished now?" he asked like a father gently correcting his child.

I could feel my lower lip starting to tremble. But I wasn't going to give him the satisfaction of thinking he'd defeated me. Instead, I punched him in the face.

Ike winced, but that was all I got out of him. He grabbed my wrist and twisted my arm behind my back. Then he used his other hand to take a handkerchief out of his pocket and dab his split lip. "You really do have your father's spunk. All I can say is that it's a good thing he's incapacitated because he'd probably be even more of a problem than Will."

"When he's feeling better, he's going to kick your ass. Both of them are," I promised.

He chuckled. "I don't think so, but I like your spirit. Now, let's go." He marched me back ahead of him toward my parents' hospital room.

Horacio had magicked up another gurney so the two FBI agents wheeled both Dad and Will into the hall. Mom had changed out of her hospital gown into something I could only assume Ike provided her. She'd probably had to change in front of the strange men.

I felt hatred for all of them boil deep inside me. But most strongly for Ike. And Masterson.

"Back entrance?" Ike asked one of the agents.

"Ambulance dock. We'll get them out in two ambulances," the agent replied.

"Excellent." Ike turned to me. "Do I have to keep your arm twisted all the way home?"

No one was coming to help. No one. "No."

He released my arm, and I rubbed it instinctively. "You're going to get into the ambulance with Will and me. Horacio will be in the ambulance with your parents. We are all going back to the estate. Once everyone has calmed down, we can have a discussion about the future."

"What discussion? You're just going to tell us how it's going to be," I said bitterly.

"See? Now you're getting it." He smiled, not even seeming to notice his split lip.

I felt bile rise in my throat, and I knew it had nothing to do with my concussion. I didn't answer him.

We took the elevator down to the ambulance dock. Two ambulances were already sitting, back doors open, waiting for us.

"You know, McKenzie, when you stop fighting the inevitable, life becomes quite easy. Just think of it like fate or destiny. You'll thank Mr. Masterson and me later," he went on as Will was loaded in one ambulance and my dad in the other.

I got into the ambulance after Will. One of the two EMTs offered me a callused hand to help me inside.

"Thank you," I said glumly, only to look up into his face and gasp in surprise.

"Shh," Shep whispered, giving me a wink.

"What's the hold up?" Ike asked, peevish.

I scooted onto the bench next to Will. "Nothing. Sorry. I stubbed my toe."

Ike rolled his eyes. "Bleeding from the head and now stubbing your toe? You're just one walking catastrophe, aren't you?"

The sound of a gun cocking answered better than I ever could. "I'm going to give you to the count of five to get your crew away from these ambulances. If you don't, I'm gonna blow your brains out. Understood?"

"Yes, ma'am," he replied. "Horacio, I think we and our friends need to take a little breather."

Horacio popped his head out of the other ambulance. "Sir?" He saw the gun and went for his jacket.

Shep pulled a shotgun from behind the ambulance door and pointed it right at Horacio. "I suggest you get to steppin'."

Horacio dropped his hand and then held both up, backing away from the ambulance slowly. "Cooper. Erdman. You need to get out of the ambulance. Slowly."

"Why the—oh." Cooper swallowed. They both held up their hands and followed Horacio, moving away from the ambulance.

"Now, just so you don't do something stupid and call the

police...." Dolly took a pair of zip-tie cuffs off her belt and cuffed Ike. "We'll let him go when we're good and ready."

"Yes, ma'am," Horacio said.

"Now, be a good little spineless asshole and throw your phone on the ground." Dolly's expression brooked no argument.

Ike slowly reached into his jacket pocket and then tossed his phone to Horacio. "Anything else?"

"Just one thing." Dolly knocked him hard on the back of the head.

For such a small woman, she was quite strong, catching Ike as he went down like a sack of potatoes.

I got out of the ambulance to help her haul him inside while Shep kept the shotgun trained on the others.

"All right, then. I'll see you soon, son." Dolly patted Shep's cheek and got into the driver's seat of the ambulance that held my parents.

"McKenzie?" Mom asked, poking her head out.

"They're friends." I smiled at her, a tear rolling down my cheek. "Oh my God, someone actually came!"

Mom grinned back. "Those are the best days." She stood and shut the ambulance doors.

Dolly took off while Shep still had the shotgun on the other three. Then he handed it to me and pointed the barrel down to Ike's temple. "If they do something stupid, or he does something stupid, shoot," he told me. Then he shut the doors and got in the driver's seat.

I looked down at Ike with raw hatred as we sped off. "Please do something stupid," I murmured.

NINE
OLD FRIENDS

Will

"Come on, buddy. It's time to wake up," a rumbling, familiar male voice said, snapping his fingers in my face.

I peeled my eyelids open and gaped. "Shep?!"

"There's our fighter," he smiled. "McKenzie was telling me how you nearly took down a man with a hundred years more training than you have."

With a groan, I sat up, rubbing the injection site on my neck. They hadn't exactly been gentle. "I was motivated."

"I'm sure you were." He sat down next to me.

It was then that I realized we were in the back of a large cargo van. Caleb was lying flat on his stomach next to me. McKenzie and Jacey were curled up together asleep in the corner.

"Is Dolly driving?" I asked.

"Sure is. Like a bat out of hell, too. After we dropped that asshole Ike in a ditch, we had to hightail it out of there pretty quick," he said. "Ma decided I should look after the troops while she gets us where we're going. Figured I could wake you up. One way or another." He grinned and cracked his knuckles.

"Glad it didn't come to that," I laughed.

"Me, too." He pulled out a water bottle and a granola bar and handed them to me.

"How'd you figure out we were in trouble?" I asked, popping the lid on the water and taking a long drink.

Shep chuckled. "We have a TV. And the Internet. Ma didn't think you'd planned to be back playing happy families with your granddad."

"We... really didn't," I confirmed.

"So, Ma decided we should pay Pa another visit. Don't think he'll ever walk a straight line again, and I'm gonna be his only son, but she got it out of him. What really happened," he said. "Real dick move on his part."

"We thought so." I closed my eyes and breathed for what felt like the first time in years. "Thank God you showed up when you did."

He shrugged. "You could have asked any trucker on the road, and they would have found me."

I grimaced. "We weren't ever allowed out alone, and we weren't given cell phones. We went straight from Ibrahim over in Europe to Ike. There just wasn't an opportunity."

Shep squeezed my shoulder. "Well, you're here now. Ma's takin' us to this vet she knows. Not an animal vet, a Desert Storm vet. He's a field medic. He's gonna take care of Caleb here."

"Good." I looked over at Caleb again and saw he was awake. "Caleb, do you want something to eat or drink?"

"Not just now. Thank you, Will," he replied politely. He looked pale.

The fact that he was polite to the man who was screwing his daughter and that he was almost white as a sheet gave me cause for concern. "Are you in pain?" I asked.

He frowned then finally nodded.

"We don't have any of the good stuff," Shep apologized. "Just Tylenol. We should have stolen some from the hospital before we left."

"It's fine," Caleb said. "Just as long as we get McKenzie and Jacey to safety, everything will be fine."

"I agree," I replied.

Caleb nodded slightly. "It's good that we agree on the important things."

"We're gettin' you to safety. Ma's friend will take care of you. If anyone has the good stuff, it'll be him," Shep said.

Unfortunately, getting to Dolly's friend and the 'good stuff' took a turn down a very bumpy gravel road.

Caleb groaned.

This woke Jacey and McKenzie. "Dad?!" McKenzie said.

"It's fine," Caleb repeated. "Everything's fine. Go back to sleep."

Jacey crawled over and held her husband's hand. "Caleb, how bad is it? Is there anything we can do?"

"Will and McKenzie's friends are taking us to someone who can help," he replied. "Everything is going to be fine."

"But you're not fine now," she fretted, stroking his hair.

The van hit a big bump, jostling all of us.

Caleb hissed.

Shep crawled over and knocked on the window between us and the driver, Dolly. "Hey, Ma? Easy on the potholes. I think Caleb's about ready to come out of his skin."

"That peckerhead Pond ain't got nothin' *but* potholes on his godforsaken land!" she shouted back. "Asshole. Just try and keep him as comfortable as possible."

"Sure thing, Ma," Shep said with a sigh. He moved back over by Jacey and Caleb. "Don't know what exactly she expects me to do...."

I went over, and so did McKenzie. We formed a helpless circle of four around Caleb. As he bit down hard on his lip, trying not to make noises of pain, I put my arm around McKenzie.

She shook it off.

Startled, I looked down at her, and she stabbed her finger into the middle of my chest. "We accept? We *accept*?! You were just going to let Ike toss us away somewhere?!" she hissed.

"What? No! He said he'd get you out. If there was a way I could guarantee that, then of course I was going to make sure you and your parents got out! I don't want you caught up in this. I never did. It's not fair to you. It's my problem," I tried to explain. "And it's nearly gotten all of you killed at least a dozen times now."

McKenzie grabbed me by the shirtfront and pulled me so close our noses almost touched. "You listen to me, William Masterson the Third. I'm not going *anywhere* without you. Ever. I love you. Don't you love me?"

"Of course I do!" It hurt that she even had a passing thought I might not. "I love you so much I couldn't bear the thought of you trapped like that."

"Get used to it. Because I'm staying. And we're not trapped anymore, anyway. We're with Dolly and Shep," she said.

Caleb gave a bitter laugh. "For now."

"Caleb! A little more hope, please? For McKenzie's sake?" Jacey chided him.

I shook my head. "No. He's right. So far, none of us have managed to *stay* safely out of my grandfather's hands."

"There's a first time for everything," Shep interrupted. "He's not the Almighty. So you can quit fightin'. We're gonna figure this out."

"See? We're going to figure it out," McKenzie echoed, scowling at me. "You don't get to give up on us, Will. Not now. Not ever."

"It's not giving up to want you safe. It's the opposite. If I can ever —" I began.

She gave me a shake. "We're a team! I didn't hallucinate you agreeing with me on that."

I sighed. "Yes, we're a team, but—"

"No buts! No take-backs! There is nothing you can say that's going to make me give up on us, Will. You're stuck with me for life," she said, giving me another shake. "Do you understand me?!"

Frustration bubbled up inside me but was instantly quashed by the desperate look in her eyes. It echoed the desperation in my heart. "You know I never *want* to be without you."

"I know," she whispered, her eyes shimmering with unshed tears. "So stop being a butthead about it."

McKenzie's tears broke me, and I wrapped her in my arms. "Okay. I'll stop being a butthead."

"Good," she sniffled.

"I'd like to revisit the 'butthead' option," Caleb muttered from the floor.

"Don't make me hit you," Jacey said. "You're starting to sound just like Dad."

Caleb stiffened, and I knew it had nothing to do with the pain. "I am not!"

"Uh-huh." Jacey smiled at us. "I think you two will do just fine."

"I think so, too," Shep agreed.

McKenzie and I looked at each other, both of us opening our mouths to say more.

Then we hit the mother of all potholes. We all levitated off the floor.

Caleb slammed back down with a loud yelp.

I ended up on my back with McKenzie on top, her knee just millimeters shy of getting me right in the balls.

Jacey and Shep bumped heads and groaned.

Dolly swore loudly enough we could hear her through the window between us. "This *motherfucker*!!!"

I was just helping McKenzie scoot off me when there was a loud **BANG**.

The van stopped abruptly.

I turned to see smoke coming from the hood of the van. "Shit, I think—"

Dolly banged her door open and came around the back of the van. She yanked the doors open, then turned to face a deserted hill.

At least, I thought it was deserted.

"Moose! You had *best* not have just killed my van!" she shouted, hands on hips.

A head with tufts of grass sticking out of it popped up on top of the hill. "That you, Dolly?"

"Who did you think it was, the National Guard? Of course it's me!" She began stomping up the hill.

It was then I saw that Moose had a large, nasty-looking rifle next to him. "Dolly, wait!"

Shep patted me on the shoulder. "Don't worry. They're old friends."

Much to my shock, and horror, Dolly marched right up to Moose, who'd gotten on his feet, and grabbed him by the ear.

"You come see what you did!" she snapped, dragging him back down the hill by his ear.

"Ouch! *Ouch!* I'll fix it, okay? I'm sure I've got another engine block running around here somewhere," Moose said.

"That ain't the problem! Problem is, I got an injured man and no way to get him to your house," Dolly complained, pulling him right up to the back of the van to see Caleb.

"Oh." Moose rubbed the impressively wild stubble on his chin. His gray hair stood out in a cloud of frizz except for the top which was flattened in a way that indicated he usually wore a baseball cap. "I'll go get my truck."

"And fix a pothole or fifty while you're at it! Lord God baby Jesus, it's like you don't even *want* visitors," Dolly said.

"I don't," Moose grumbled but trudged off with his rifle just the same.

Dolly sat down on the back bumper with her arms folded. "One of these days, I'm gonna come here, and he'll be wearin' a tinfoil hat."

"Pretty sure he's got one in his kitchen," Shep chuckled.

She reached back and swatted her son. "Don't sass your elders."

"Sorry, Ma," Shep replied contritely. But his lips were still twitching behind her back.

Caleb had stopped making noise, but I could tell from the slight tremble in his body that he was in a lot of pain. I tried distracting

McKenzie from it, but she'd seen it, too, and wouldn't stop staring at her father. No doubt we were both willing him to get through it. And praying Moose really did have 'the good stuff.'

Jacey laid next to him, holding his hand.

Dolly glanced back every once in a while as the minutes passed and cursed Moose under her breath.

Shep sat up suddenly. "There he is!"

Sure enough, a beat-up, yet high-riding, pickup truck came lumbering down the dirt road, mowing over potholes as though they didn't even exist.

Dolly jumped down off the bumper. "Took you long enough!"

"I had to pick up a few things." Moose descended from the cab and fished around the back seat. He came up with a cloth bag that he brought into the back of the van. He knelt down next to Caleb and zipped the back open to reveal a few syringes and a vial of very pale yellow liquid. "Morphine," he explained to us as he readied a syringe.

"Thank you," Jacey said softly.

Moose nodded. "What happened to him?"

"He was burned a bit and hit by a bunch of shrapnel when a bomb went off," Jacey explained. She held up her own bandaged arm. "He jumped on top of me so I didn't get hurt."

"Good man," Moose said. "You'll feel a bit of a pinch, but I'll bet that's the least of your worries right now." He injected Caleb efficiently and without a moment of hesitation.

Very quickly, Caleb relaxed.

"There we go. All right, we've gotta get him in the flatbed. I see two strapping men here about to volunteer for duty." Moose's tone brooked no argument.

"Yes, sir," Shep replied.

"Absolutely," I said, reluctantly letting go of McKenzie so I could help.

"Sir," Moose added.

"What?" I responded, confused.
"Son, you call me 'sir,'" Moose said firmly.
I straightened up. "Of course, sir."
"Good. Now let's get this man back to the house."

TEN

MOOSE

McKenzie

We got to Moose's house without incident. I really had been expecting a bunker with a tinfoil baseball cap hanging by the door. But it was really just a good-sized farm house set back near a pond. Old farm equipment was scattered around, rusting in an overgrown field. Even though we didn't have that sort of thing back home, our neighbors did, and it made me nostalgic.

Moose swung open the front door of the weathered old farm-house, and Will and Shep carried Dad inside. "Take him through that door there," Moose said, pointing. "Closest to the kitchen and my supply cabinet.

Mom followed right after them, but it turned out it was a small room, so we couldn't all crowd inside.

Will stepped out and put an arm around me again, and this time I didn't shake him off, even though I was still a little mad at him. *Big dumb hero complex.*

My worry must have shown on my face because Dolly came to stand beside us. "He'll be fine, honey. Moose is an expert in this sort of thing."

In fact, Moose was already changing Dad's dressings, checking the wounds underneath. From what I could see, Dad had taken a lot of damage.

"It's not as bad as it looks," Moose said, as though hearing my unspoken concern.

"You're sure?" Mom asked, sitting on the very edge of the bed and stroking Dad's hair. "It looks awful."

"Yeah, but most of it didn't get into the muscle tissue, and it doesn't look as though they had to go down to the bone, so all in all, good for... what's his name?" Moose looked at Mom briefly.

"Caleb," Mom said. "His name is Caleb."

"Right. Caleb. You're doing all right, Caleb," Moose told him.

"Good to know." Dad's voice was muffled by the pillow.

Moose worked methodically until he'd completely changed the dressings then stood. "We'll let him rest now. I'm assuming you'll be taking the chair there missus...?"

"Just call me Jacey," Mom said. "And yes, I'll take the chair."

"We can sit outside," I suggested. "That way—"

"You're going to go get some rest." Mom's tone was no-nonsense. The one that was impossible to argue with.

I pouted. "But—"

"You know Will there is still fightin' off drugs," Dolly said.

"Again," Will grumbled.

"He could probably use the rest," Dolly continued.

I drooped, looking at Will, torn between him and my parents.

He rubbed my back. "Don't worry about it. I'm fine. I'll just go lay down on the couch. You won't be far away."

"After you drink a shitton of water," Moose said, grabbing Will by the arm and dragging him into the kitchen. "Gotta flush those drugs out."

"McKenzie, go stay with Will. Please. Someone needs to watch over him," Mom murmured once he was out of earshot.

I glanced at Dad then looked worriedly at Will. I'd never forgive myself if he ended up having a bad reaction to the drug and no one was there to help him in time. The very idea made me sick to my stomach. "Okay. You're right. I know you'll take good care of Dad."

"Always," Dad mumbled into his pillow, just loud enough to be heard.

Shep chuckled. "You Killeens and your significants. It's really somethin' to see."

"I wish you'd get a significant. Grandbabies don't make themselves," Dolly muttered.

As I tried not to laugh at Shep's dilemma, Will downed a glass of water. Moose refilled it, and he downed another.

When Moose refilled the glass again, Will's eyebrows shot up, but he obediently forced it down. He held up a hand. "Sorry, sir, I think that's all I can do for now."

"That'll do for now." Moose set the empty glass on the counter like it was a threat then ushered Will to the nearby stairs. "Bedroom on the left with the blue quilt. Never thought my parents leaving me this big damn house was ever going to come in handy."

I trotted up behind Will. "Thank you, sir."

Moose nodded. "A man should always do the right thing. Bathroom's on the right when he needs it."

"Thanks," I said again.

The room with the blue quilt on the bed was actually quite quaint. It was small, but it had a nice, bright window with a seat underneath. An armoire next to it held extra bedding, and the low dresser along the opposite wall was filled with men's and women's clothing in every shape and size.

Whatever else Moose might be, the man was prepared.

"Mind if I lie down?" Will asked, sitting on the edge of the bed.

"Of course you need to lie down, silly!" I went over and pushed on his chest to force him down on the bed. He laughed and didn't fight me.

I plumped up a pillow behind his head then went to the other side of the bed and climbed in, snuggling up next to him. We linked hands over his abs.

"So... when Moose said 'a man should always do the right thing...'" he broached the subject.

I rolled my eyes. I knew it was going to be a problem the second the words left Moose's mouth. "Will, if you try to back out of our agreement or tell me how justified you were when you tried to make that deal with Ike, I'm going to scream."

"But—"

"I know you were just trying to do the right thing. But it wasn't the right thing, was it?" I chided him. "It was the wrong thing, and you know it."

He made a noncommittal sound.

"Will!" I smacked his abs, and he winced.

"Careful, I've had a lot of water," he reminded me.

"Tough. I swear, if we ever have to have this conversation again, I am going to knee you right in the balls. You're my person. We stick together, no matter what." I leaned up on my arm so he could see how serious I was.

He sighed. "I'll never do it again."

It wasn't an admission of wrongdoing, but I'd take it. "Promise me."

"I swear, if we ever get into that situation again, I will not try to bargain with Ike or my grandfather. I won't let them take you away from me," he said, sincere.

"Good. Now I want to put the subject to bed," I sniffed. "I don't want to talk about it again. Ever."

"Okay, okay." He squeezed my hand. "Let's get some rest before I need to spend seven hundred years in the bathroom."

I couldn't help it. I giggled.

"You think it's funny now..." he muttered. Then he gave me a soft kiss and closed his eyes.

I smiled and laid my head on his shoulder. Something inside me decided that everything was going to be okay.

WHEN I WOKE UP, Will was gone.

I sat straight up, my head whipping around. "Will?"

"Bathroom," Moose said, sticking his head into the room. It was dark outside, but Moose had installed nightlights in our room and down the hall. Probably in the bathroom as well.

"Oh." I relaxed. "Hello, sir. Thanks for taking us in and taking care of us. I know we're probably intruding on your peace."

"Eh, Dolly's always intruding on my peace. Makes life fun." He smiled fondly.

"How long have you known Dolly?" I asked, curious.

Moose chuckled. "We grew up together. Her family owned the farm next door. I took her to prom. But she had big dreams of seeing the world, and I had big dreams of joining the military and saving it, just like my father. Some things they don't tell ya goin' in." His smile faded.

"I'm sorry. I didn't mean to bring up bad memories." I looked around. "Where are Dolly and Shep?"

"Well, not in your room, for sure." He grinned again. "Shep's down the hall. Dolly's with me. Even old people like a little company once in a while."

I laughed. "You're not old, and neither is Dolly. You're both too feisty."

"I'm glad you think so. But we are old. This is probably our last rescue mission. Gotta say, never expected Dolly to bring me people, though. Usually, it's dogs she finds on the road. I'm practically an animal sanctuary sometimes. But they've all been adopted for now."

"You don't ever keep any?" I asked.

Moose shrugged. "One every once in a while. Usually a poor, disabled, not-so-pretty-lookin' one. The ones nobody will adopt."

"That's sad. I mean, not for you. I'll bet you're a great pet dad. I mean that no one wants to adopt them," I said.

"It's the way of the world, McKenzie. Most people don't want broken things," he replied with a touch of sadness.

I got the feeling he was talking about himself. At least a little bit.

But I didn't say anything. Moose didn't seem the type to want me to comment on that revelation. I just nodded.

Will came back then, blinking at Moose. "Hello, sir."

"Don't get your undies in a bundle. I'm just here sayin' hi. I figured when I heard her wakin' up and you not being there she might panic," Moose said.

"Oh. Right." Will relaxed.

Given everything we'd been through, I couldn't blame him for puffing up like that on Moose.

"Also wanted to apologize," Moose went on. "Dolly and I are goin' to be havin' relations. Might get a bit loud. You're welcome to the earplugs in that drawer there. Oh, and I ain't got a problem if you want to have relations in the guest bed. It's probably been a bit for you kids."

Will coughed. "'Kids'?"

"Son, when you're my age, everyone's a kid." Moose gave us a wave. "Can't keep Dolly waitin' too long." He walked back down the hall.

Will shut the door and came back to bed, this time stripping down to his boxers and pulling back the blankets. "I think it might officially be bedtime."

"Do you think we'll need the earplugs?" I asked, taking off my sundress. I took off my bra as well, and he raised his eyebrows, only to sigh in disappointment when I grabbed an oversized T-shirt from the dresser.

"I'm sure we'll want them, yes," he replied. "Dolly doesn't strike me as a quiet woman."

I laughed. "I don't think there's anything quiet about Dolly." I rummaged in the drawer Moose had indicated and came up with two sets of squishy yellow earplugs. I put on the T-shirt, then brought the earplugs to the bed.

He looked at them, rolled them between his fingers, then set them back down. "I want to be able to hear you."

"We'll be asleep," I pointed out.

"Yes." He stroked my cheek. "But I want to hear you breathe."

I felt heat flood my cheeks. "I like hearing your heartbeat," I admitted.

Will's smile warmed me to my toes. "I guess we're not using these, then."

"I guess not." I picked up our earplugs and set them on the window seat.

He pulled the covers back on my side, inviting me in.

I wriggled into bed, and he tucked the blankets around me after I cuddled into his side.

"Honeybee?" he whispered just as I was getting drowsy.

"Uh-huh?" I yawned, shifting so I was lying on his chest with my ear right over his heart.

"I think we should have 'relations' soon."

I snorted. "One track mind."

"You know it," he said.

"But...."

"But?" he asked hopefully.

"I think we should, too," I agreed.

ELEVEN
A BRAND NEW START

Will

Relations would have to wait. The next morning, Moose and Dolly pulled us together for a meeting outside Caleb and Jacey's room. We all sat on beat-up folding chairs.

From what McKenzie and I had heard the night before, I was impressed that Dolly could sit at all.

"So, we've got ourselves a situation," Moose said.

"Please, dear God, tell me the situation is that Masterson hung himself in prison," Caleb called from his bed.

Moose grimaced. "No such luck, I'm afraid. The situation I'm talkin' about is how to keep you out of Masterson's hands."

"I think we're off his radar," I said. "I mean, way out here in the middle of nowhere. Where are we, anyway?"

"Outside Melrose," Moose responded, naming a Minnesota town north of St. Cloud. It was about an hour and a half northwest of Minnetonka, where the Masterson Estate was.

Caleb gave a low whistle. "Pretty far off the beaten path. At least Masterson's beaten path."

"Yeah, but he's not going to stop lookin' for you," Moose said.

"We've gotta be smart about this. First thing I gotta do, and I should have done it right when you got here, is see if any of you are tagged."

"Tagged?" Jacey echoed. "What do you mean, 'tagged'?"

"Just like it sounds. Subdermal tracking device," Moose replied.

My blood froze in my veins. "Shit."

"You think you might be tagged?" Moose asked.

"I feel sick," McKenzie murmured.

I put an arm around her, though I couldn't say I didn't feel the same. "I don't know if we are," I said. "I mean, I wouldn't be surprised at all if *I* am. But I'd be willing to bet money Caleb and Jacey are."

"He always knew where we were," Jacey whispered, going pale. "Always."

"Right. Well, lucky for us, I keep this property covered with signal disruption, but they might have been able to follow your tracker up to the property. That could be a problem," Moose said.

"We don't want to get you killed!" McKenzie burst out. "We should leave." She looked up at me. "So many people keep dying...."

I nodded. "You're our friends. We can't bring Grandfather's wrath down on you. If you give us an hour or two to figure out where we can go—"

"Pfft." Dolly shook her head. "A bit late for that now. We're in it up to our necks. Now, you listen to Moose, and we'll see what we can figure out."

"Okay." I squeezed McKenzie's shoulder, offering her comfort while she looked completely crestfallen.

"I'm gonna use a scanner on all of you. Then we're gonna pack up and take off. I've got property near Grand Marais," Moose said. "Not in my real name. Not like this place."

"That sounds very well thought out." Caleb complimented him.

"You gotta be prepared. You never know what's gonna happen." Moose stood and got what looked like a wand they used at the airport out of a cupboard. He turned to McKenzie. "You first."

McKenzie got up and spread her arms and legs, allowing Moose to wand her more easily.

I scowled when the wand beeped around her hand.

"That's where my IV was in the hospital," she murmured. "Oh my God."

"There are slippery assholes in this world," Moose said. "Since there's no raised bump under your skin here, I'm assumin' they got it between the bones. Means it's gonna to be a bitch to get out." He sighed. "But we're gonna have to."

My chest swelled with pride when my honeybee simply set her jaw and nodded. "Do what you have to do."

"See, why can't you find a nice girl with big lady balls like that?" Dolly asked Shep.

Shep just laughed good-naturedly.

"I'm gonna wand the others first, then we'll start gettin' trackers out," Moose said. "Okay, Will, you're up."

I kissed McKenzie on the cheek then stood in front of him.

My tracker, as it turned out, was in my left calf.

"Yep, embedded in the muscle, if I'm not mistaken," Moose muttered. "Another fun minor surgery happenin' today."

"I had a football injury there once. Someone got me with their cleats." I shook my head angrily. "He used it as an opportunity to chip me like a dog."

"He sure did." Moose took the wand into Caleb and Jacey's bedroom. Both of them had trackers in their left arms.

Moose motioned to McKenzie. "You and me are goin' in the kitchen."

She swallowed and walked with him into the kitchen.

Luckily, it was an open kitchen, so we were all able to see what Moose was doing. Still, it wasn't enough for me, and I wandered in and took her other hand. "You can squeeze my hand off if you need to. I know it might hurt."

McKenzie gave me a nervous smile.

"I'm gonna numb the area. It shouldn't hurt too much," Moose reassured us. "And Will, you gotta stay outta my way."

"Yes, sir," I replied.

Moose took a syringe of something else and slowly made small injections around the area of her hand where he'd be performing the surgery. Then he pressed down on the site. "Can you feel that?"

"Just a little pressure, but nothing else," she said.

"Good. That's what we want." Moose got out a kit and pulled out a scalpel. "I'll probably have to stitch you up when I'm done. I'll make sure the area's still numb."

"Okay. Thank you," she responded.

I didn't want to watch. But I had to. I couldn't let her go through it alone.

It took what seemed like forever, but finally he removed the tracker with tweezers.

"What do we do with it now?" I asked, glowering at the small device.

"This." He opened a drawer, took out a meat cleaver, and slammed it down on the tracker. It was very satisfying to watch.

Then he expertly stitched up McKenzie's hand and bandaged it. "Not too bad, McKenzie?"

"No. I didn't even have to squeeze Will's hand off." She gave a nervous grin.

"I'm sure he appreciates that. Speaking of which, pants off and up on the counter you go," he said after sterilizing the space.

My tracker, as it turned out, was very deeply embedded in the muscle.

"Guess Grandfather was afraid I'd run off on him and wanted to make sure I couldn't." I grunted while he put in a third round of numbing injections and kept fishing for the tracker.

"Your grandfather is an asshole." Moose finally came up with the tracker. "Jesus fuckin' Christ. That's gonna be sore for a while. Here, McKenzie, you do the honors. I've gotta start stitching him back up."

She took the tracker and slammed the meat cleaver down on it. Then she did it two more times.

"Okay, it's dead. You can stop any time now," he said, working on my stitches.

"It's not nearly dead enough," she muttered but stopped beating on it.

"I love you, too," I chuckled, trying not to wince when Moose hit an area that wasn't quite numb enough anymore.

He tapped my thigh. "None of that manly stoic bullshit, now. You need to be able to walk on out of here in the next couple of hours. You tell me when it hurts so I can numb it some more. Understand?"

"Yes, sir," I said contritely.

"What he said," McKenzie agreed, glaring at me.

Moose numbed the area again then finished stitching me up. He put a dressing on the area. "All right, Caleb and Jacey. I'm comin' in there next. You hop on down, Will. Try not to put too much weight on it for the time being."

I nodded and carefully got down from the counter.

McKenzie hugged me. "I'm glad that's over. Watching was awful. He really had to dig in there."

I hugged her back. "I felt the same way when he was doing your hand."

She snorted. "He didn't have to dig in my hand as much as he had to in your leg."

"Still, I didn't like it." I kissed the top of her head.

"I'd say go pack, but I don't think any of you have anythin' but the clothes on your backs," Dolly said. She looked at Shep. "Go get our bags. There's a second bag in Moose's room. He already packed."

"Sure, Ma. I'll be right back." Shep took the stairs two at a time.

I waited impatiently for Moose to finish, praying Ike hadn't already tracked the signal to this area.

Shep didn't come back downstairs right away.

"Is Shep okay?" I asked Dolly.

She frowned. "Shep! What's keepin' ya?"

"Well, Ma, we got a problem," Shep replied from upstairs.

"What problem?" she asked.

"There's a bunch of men with guns outside, and one of them's got their rifle pointed right at me," he said.

I couldn't believe he sounded so calm. I was not calm. "Fuuuuuuuck...."

"Oh God," McKenzie whispered. "We've got to get my parents out of here!"

"Moose, you done?" Dolly asked, just as calm as her son. "We got World War Three building up outside, according to my son."

He came out of the bedroom holding a tracker, dropped it on the floor, and crushed it under his foot. "Still gotta get Jacey."

Someone banged on the front door. "Open up! We don't want to shoot, but we will if you don't hand them over!"

"I hate being interrupted while I'm workin'," Moose complained. "You three might want to get behind the counter." Then he took what looked like a TV remote out of his back pocket, flipped off a protective cover, and pressed a button.

The front porch exploded.

Glass, wood, and sheetrock dust rained down around us. The counter did provide a good barrier, however, and Dolly, McKenzie, and I did not get hit by any nasty shrapnel.

"Bet those fuckers weren't expecting that," Moose said with a slight snicker.

The insurgent team backed off, and Shep came pelting down the stairs, holding three duffel bags. "What now?" he asked.

"I gotta get that tracker outta Jacey, or it ain't gonna matter what we do now," Moose replied in frustration. "Will, Shep, you get Caleb and take him to the basement. Dolly, Jacey, McKenzie, you follow them down. We're gonna have to go to the bunker for a bit."

"Bunker?" Dolly responded. She chuckled. "Aren't you full of surprises?"

Moose just grinned. "All right, people, let's get this show on the road before they regroup."

Dolly, Jacey, and McKenzie each took a duffel bag while Shep and I went and lifted Caleb out of the bed as carefully as we could. To his credit, he didn't make a sound as we carried him down the stairs.

Moose went to a sturdy-looking cabinet and pressed a cinder block on the wall next to it. The cabinet swung outward with a loud creak.

"You always were good with your hands," Dolly said fondly, preceding us all down the long corridor behind the cabinet. The way was lit with LED lights, and there was only one direction to go, so it wasn't difficult to follow Dolly even with Caleb suspended between Shep and me.

"Love you, too," Moose mumbled under his breath and took the rear after Jacey and McKenzie, closing the cabinet behind us.

TWELVE
THE BUNKER

McKenzie

Like everything about Moose's surroundings, the way was well-lit, as was the bunker beyond. We walked for what must have been at least a mile until we got to a large, one-room bunker stocked to the gills with everything that would be needed for Doomsday. Food. Flak vests. Guns. Water. Everything.

Will and Shep set Dad down on a cot on his belly. Dad only winced once.

"All right." Moose wandered over to Mom and pulled her over to sit in a chair. "Gotta get that tracker out of you before we can go anywhere."

Mom nodded and offered her arm.

He took his kit out of his shirt and went to work. After several minutes, the tracker was out and crushed under the butt of a gun, and Mom was stitched back up.

"We're gonna stock up here a bit, then we're goin' up that ladder and into the woods. I've got a truck and a Jeep stowed out there, and there's a dirt road leadin' out of the woods to the other side of the property. We'll get out right under their noses," Moose said.

"Sounds great," Dolly replied. "What do we need to pack?"

Moose started pointing at various guns and the flak vests. "We need to be armed, just in case."

"All right." She began expertly putting together sets of gear and handing them around to all of us.

"We're gonna lay a vest over Caleb," Moose explained. "Best we can do to protect him."

Mom made a concerned noise.

"Best thing you can do for him now is shoot straight," Dolly said, handing Mom her gear.

I put on my vest and did the best I could stowing the guns around my body. Dolly sighed and rearranged them. She had to do the same for Will and Mom.

"Civilians. I've got me an injured man and three civilians," Moose lamented, expertly putting himself together.

Dolly and Shep were no slouches. Moose didn't need to correct them.

Moose took a deep breath then went up the ladder. He pushed open a hatch and looked around.

"All right. Let's be quickish. McKenzie, you'll need to help Will with your father this time. I'll need Shep to be ready to open fire," Moose said.

I nodded and went with Will to get Dad.

This time, Dad made himself sit up then stand unaided.

"Dad!" I objected.

"It's a ladder. I won't have you falling down a ladder from dragging around my useless ass," Dad said between his teeth. "You can carry me after, if you must, but I'm climbing that thing myself."

"Good plan. If you can do it, that would really help the cause," Moose replied before Will or I could say anything.

Dad nodded and headed for the ladder, going up right behind Moose. It was painful to watch. His whole body shook.

"Caleb..." Mom whispered, clasping her hands under her chin.

"Come on up, love. I'm doing fine, and Moose seems to think the coast is clear." Dad reached behind him, though I knew it must have hurt like hell, and still managed to smile at Mom.

Mom didn't hesitate. She went right to him.

"There we go. Okay, Dolly, you get in the middle there then McKenzie and Will. Shep, you take up the rear," Moose said.

We quickly shuffled into order. Moose climbed out of the hatch first, followed by my parents, followed by Dolly, followed by Will and me, and then Shep.

Dad leaned heavily on Mom once we made it out. Without a word, Will and I ran forward and scooped Dad up between us. He was muscular from all the farm labor he'd done over the years, so it turned out Mom had to help on my end. I wasn't a wilting flower by any stretch of the imagination, but Dad weighed a ton.

"This way." Moose shut the hatch, which made it look like just another grass-covered bit of dirt, and then led us deeper into the woods.

Shep and Dolly were alert, ready for anything, as was Moose. It made me start listening to every tiny sound, wondering if it was a sign of approaching assassins.

It didn't take long to get to the truck and the Jeep. They had camouflage mesh thrown over them, which Moose dragged off. He had us lay Dad in the back of the Jeep. Mom got in the back with him so he laid with his head in her lap.

"Shep, Dolly, you take the Jeep," Moose said, reaching under the wheel well and throwing her the keys.

Dolly caught them and got in the driver's seat.

"Will, McKenzie, get in the back of the truck and keep your heads down. I'm driving," Moose ordered.

We didn't need to be told twice. Will and I climbed into the back of the truck, then Will leaned over me protectively, the way I imagined Dad must have done for Mom before the explosion that tore up his back.

"If you get hurt, I'm never going to forgive you, Will Masterson the Third," I warned him.

"I'll keep that in mind," he snorted.

Moose got in the truck and fired up the engine. He weaved through some trees. I could hear the Jeep following behind.

Finally, after a long, bumpy time, the ride smoothed out, and I realized we must be on some official road.

"There, that wasn't so bad, was it?" Moose asked.

Will started to sit up.

"Did I tell you to pop your head up yet?" Moose said sternly.

He folded himself back down on top of me.

"So, we're going to Grand Marais?" I asked about the northern town situated on Lake Superior.

"We sure are. Just outside. I've got some property and a cabin," Moose replied.

"My parents said they went there. That they liked it. It's supposed to be pretty," I said conversationally.

"I ain't worried about pretty, McKenzie. I'm worried about safe." Moose went silent after that.

Will and I lay curled and cramped together in the back seat for at least an hour, also holding the silence. Finally, blessedly, Moose said, "I reckon you can sit up now."

We shot up like gophers out of a hole, both a bit sweaty.

Moose chuckled. "You two look like you've been going at it."

"No such luck," Will muttered under his breath.

I elbowed him. "We're very grateful to you, sir. And I'm very sorry about your house. That must be your childhood home, and you blew off the front porch!"

"Oh, I blew off more than that. Once we were in the bunker, I blew the whole thing to kingdom come. Let them sort *that* out." Moose gave a dark laugh.

My jaw dropped. "Oh my God."

"I'll compensate you as soon as I can," Will said, sounding apologetic. "You shouldn't have had to sacrifice all that for us."

Moose shrugged. "It's just a house. I always knew I'd be blowin' it up someday. Someone's always comin' for ya, you know?"

"Yes, we know something about that," Will murmured.

Even though I was sweaty, I leaned into Will, and he put an arm around me. "So, how do you handle a life on the run?"

"Two words. Be prepared. Just like the Scouts," Moose said.

"We weren't prepared," Will replied. "Now we're scrambling to catch up."

"Well, that's why you've got me. I ain't no slouch in the preparedness department. And you got me Dolly. I'd have blown up a hundred houses for her." Moose smiled fondly in the rearview mirror. "She's a hard one to hold onto. Free spirit."

"She's one of a kind, I'll agree with you there." I grinned. Curiosity ate at me, and finally I blurted, "Why doesn't she just stay? She clearly likes you very much. Does Shep not like you?"

"McKenzie..." Will murmured.

Moose chuckled. "Shep's as much my son as he can be without bein' blood. Nah, I've got some really bad PTSD and night terrors. When they get bad, I've pushed them both away cuz I don't want them to get hurt. Last time, the fight was pretty brutal. I wasn't sure she'd ever come back. Of course, by the time I was sure she was gone for good, I figured out what an idiot I'd been. I thought it was too late. But now here she is. I'm not fuckin' it up again, I can tell you that right now."

"I'm sorry about your PTSD and night terrors," I said, feeling for the man. "And I'm glad Dolly's back in your life. Even if she did bring us all along for the ride."

"She brought me a mountain lion that had been hit by a truck once. Never thought she could bring me anythin' more interestin' than that. But I was underestimatin' her." Moose smiled.

I laughed. Will joined in.

"So, Dolly's told me a little bit. Is it true you both came outta that lovely Jacey woman in the Jeep?" Moose asked, confusion in his tone.

Will and I glanced at each other awkwardly. "Yes," Will finally said. "I was born thirty years ago, and Jacey was my surrogate. Donor egg. My father's sperm. So if you're thinking we're related or doing something gross...."

"Nah. I mean, it ain't normal, but nothin' is." Moose looked at me. "And you're nineteen?"

"It's not that big of an age difference," I mumbled, blushing.

Moose slapped his knee and laughed. "Well, I know there's been bigger ones. And you live in that hifalutin' society, Will. You got them ninety-year-old men with them eighteen-year-old girls. You two are practically tame by comparison."

"I won't argue with you there," Will said with a wince of distaste. "I've always wondered about those couples, but they both seem perfectly happy."

"It's a business trade, you know that. She gets money. He gets... well, we know what he gets. I even hear sometimes it's the other way around. Older lady. Younger guy," Moose replied.

"There's definitely a few of those," Will confirmed.

Moose let out more loud guffaws. "I'm tryin' to picture it. Scratch that, I'm tryin' *not* to picture it. You all hifalutin' folks get wound up about the weirdest things then do stuff like that. Makes no damn sense."

"True." Will played with my hair, idly twirling it around his fingers.

It made my scalp tingle.

"How many rooms are there in this cabin? Are we all bunking up together?" he asked.

"It's a big cabin. Plenty of space. I guess they call them 'lake homes,'" Moose said in his best rich-people impression.

I laughed. Will just rolled his eyes.

"Don't you go rollin' your eyes at your betters, Will Masterson," Moose scolded him.

Will cringed. "Sorry, sir."

"That's better. What I'm tryin' to say is if you want to rock the paint off the walls, you'll have your own room to do it in. Which I think was the question you were meanin' to ask," Moose said.

With a self-conscious cough, Will admitted, "That was the question, yes."

I swatted him. "Ugh, men! Is that all you think about?!"

Will and Moose looked at each other. "Well," Moose said, "most of the time, yeah."

"I'm surrounded." I groaned, dropping my head into my hands.

Will kissed the back of my neck then rubbed my arms. "You would have asked the same question as soon as we got there."

"What makes you think that?" I asked, frowning.

"Because I know you've been dying to take some paint off the walls. Just as much as I have," he whispered in my ear.

Now it wasn't just my scalp tingling. I tingled all over. "It's only been two days," I said, but I sounded weak to my own ears.

"I agree. We should have done it the night before we saw Grandfather. But neither of us was in the mood. Hindsight's twenty-twenty." He tucked my hair behind my ear and kissed my temple.

It wasn't fair that he got to be so composed while I was becoming a messy puddle. Then I watched him shift in his seat, barely able to hide a raging boner.

Not so composed after all.

"H-how much longer to Grand Marais?" I asked, licking my lips.

"Another three hours," Moose said.

This was going to be the longest ride of my life!

THIRTEEN
CHIPPING THE PAINT OFF

Will

I stroked McKenzie's hair while she slept against my shoulder. I would have had her put her head in my lap, but that would have been a recipe for disaster. I was already having a hard time. Literally.

"You look like you're havin' fun," Moose snickered from the front seat.

With a grimace, I shifted again, trying to tell my dick to calm down. But McKenzie was so close, and I could smell her unique, light scent. It was a losing battle.

He kept chuckling. "You should always get a woman who makes you feel like a teenager again. Dolly and me, we're practically sixteen again."

I tried not to think of Moose and Dolly in bed together. "Er... that's good."

"You're a bit uptight. You need to loosen up. People have sex, and they enjoy it. It's not a crime," he said.

"True," I reluctantly agreed. "I just don't come from a background where we talk about it openly."

He snorted. "No kiddin'. But you're gonna be in the same cabin we are, and I don't think you're gonna be any quieter than Dolly and me, so I figure ain't no shame in being honest."

"That is... also true," I conceded. Once I got my hands on McKenzie again, there wasn't going to be anything quiet happening in that bedroom.

"You need condoms?" he asked, making me choke.

"N-no. McKenzie has it... taken care of," I explained. "But thank you."

"She ain't carryin' birth control with her," he said, concerned. "You know, if a woman misses a dose—"

I rubbed a hand over my face. "She has an IUD. It lasts five years."

"Oh. Nice." He nodded his approval. "That's the way to go. Dolly's been through menopause, so that's great for me."

"That sounds... great...." I hadn't ever felt this uncomfortable in my entire life.

Moose laughed. "I can hear you bitin' your tongue."

I coughed self-consciously. "That's not... I'm... it's...."

"Relax. We're just passin' the time." He glanced at me in the rearview mirror. "You love her?"

"More than my life," I responded without hesitation.

"That's good. It's good to have a person like that." He stared off into the distance. "Maybe I can patch things up with Dolly, and we can make a go of it. A real one."

"That sounds like an excellent plan," I said enthusiastically.

He smiled. "I ain't gonna fuck it up this time."

"Of course not," I agreed. "You've grown and matured. If we're lucky, none of us make the same mistakes."

"Well, at least you're old enough to understand the luck part," he chuckled.

I shifted again, this time with embarrassment. "Sorry. I don't mean to be patronizing."

"You mean well. That's what counts." He looked in the rearview mirror again, this time past me.

I supposed he was looking at the Jeep, which held his precious Dolly.

He frowned.

My pulse went from placid to panicked with that one expression. "Are we being followed?"

"Nah. Dolly's giving me the signal she wants to stop for gas or somethin'. Maybe a pee break. But them stations have cameras...." He didn't sound happy.

"Can we make it without getting gas?" I asked.

Moose sighed. "No." He waved back then watched the side of the road for an exit sign that also indicated the presence of a gas station.

"Maybe McKenzie and I should stay in the truck?" I suggested.

"You're gonna wanna pee. Besides, they've been on my property and probably got Dolly and Shep's pictures from hospital security. It ain't gonna matter at this point." He exited the highway and pulled into a gas station.

I gently nudged McKenzie awake. "Bathroom break."

She yawned and stretched. Then she looked around. "Don't these places have cameras?" she whispered as though we might be overheard by one of them.

"We're gonna make this as quick as possible. Get to the bathroom and get right back," Moose said as he hopped out of the truck.

"So, no gas station bathroom sex, then," she whispered naughtily in my ear just as I was stepping out of the truck.

My dick twitched with the delicious memory of when we had done just that, and I gave her a dirty look. "Thanks for that."

McKenzie grinned and raced into the station. I was hot on her heels.

"Don't even think about it," Dolly said as we weaved through the shelves toward the bathrooms.

"Think about what?" McKenzie asked innocently.

"There isn't time. Now, do your business and get back in the truck." Dolly was handing armloads of groceries to Shep.

"We weren't actually going to do anything," I said.

"Uh-huh. Your pants are tellin' a different story." Dolly snorted.

McKenzie looked down. "Will!"

I clasped my hands as casually as possible over the danger zone. "That's just a biological reaction."

"Uh-huh." Dolly pointed at the restrooms. "Hurry it up. And no funny business."

I sighed and ushered McKenzie ahead of me to the bathroom, seeing her all to the ladies' room door. Then I went one door over, wishing we did have the time and freedom to do something about our mutual predicament. I knew McKenzie wasn't unaffected, though I envied that her situation wasn't so blatantly obvious.

I thought about giving myself some one-handed relief, but I decided against it. All I needed was for Moose or Shep to wander in and tell me I was wasting time.

When I got out of the bathroom, I waited for McKenzie. She walked out looking just as frustrated as I felt.

"We'd better get to that cabin soon," she grumbled. "I'm about ready to lose my mind!"

"Me, too." I put an arm around her, and we went back to the truck together.

Moose was already in the driver's seat and ready to go. "I was afraid you decided to shake the tile in there anyway."

"No such luck," I said. "How much longer?"

"About an hour. You might as well take a nap. Both of you. It'll make the time go by faster," he said.

I helped McKenzie into the back of the truck. Her fine ass waved in my face briefly, and I wondered if it was possible to die of sexual frustration.

As soon as I was in, Moose put the truck in gear. "Let's go." He pulled out of the station.

I glanced out the back window and saw Dolly was right on our tail.

"Nap," Moose insisted when the silence stretched out in the cab of the truck.

It was as good a plan as any. I wrapped my arm around McKenzie, snuggling her against my chest, her head nestled beneath my chin. When her breathing evened out, my eyelids drooped. Soon, we were asleep together.

THE TRUCK THRASHING ABRUPTLY WOKE me up. It was full dark, and we were driving without the headlights on.

I grabbed the back of the passenger seat while McKenzie, now also awake, grabbed me. "Moose?!"

"Don't worry about it. I've got light markers on the trees on either side," he replied without any concern.

I peered more closely at our surroundings, and, sure enough, there were dimly lit solar lights indicating the sides of the... road?

"Is this your driveway?" I asked, holding McKenzie tightly. I wasn't sure it would help all the bouncing around, but I figured it couldn't hurt.

"That it is. Long way in from the road. I didn't want to use the headlights, just in case." He made a sudden turn, and McKenzie and I tumbled into the door. "Hang on."

"You usually say that *before* the turn," I muttered, rubbing my elbow.

Moose scoffed. "Rich kids are such big babies."

"I don't agree," I responded. "I'm just saying—"

"Moose, are we there yet? Caleb's whiter than mashed potatoes." Dolly's voice came over a walkie-talkie.

I hadn't even realized we had one.

He swore and called her back. "Fifteen minutes."

"I swear, Moose, why must every property you own have a road so full of holes it could have survived a bombing!" Dolly chided him.

"Keeps people out." He was peevish, yet practical.

"Don't you take that tone with me," Dolly said. "I ain't the one with holes in my road so big one of 'em's gonna swallow this Jeep."

"Then we'll go fishin' for it." He had lost his tone, however.

"Uh-huh." Dolly closed the channel, and the static stopped.

"Dad's going to be okay, right?" McKenzie asked.

Moose nodded. "He'll be just fine. Gonna need to give him more morphine, but last time I checked, his wounds were clean. No infections."

"Okay." McKenzie looked up at me in the low dashboard lighting. "I want to make sure my parents are settled before we do anything."

"Of course," I agreed. "They're your parents. They're definitely a higher priority than... chipping paint off the walls. We'll have plenty of time for that."

She smiled at me. Then we hit another pothole and bumped foreheads.

"Ow," we said at the same time.

"Ugh. You're both big babies," Moose tsked. We rounded another corner, narrowly missed a skinny little tree that had obviously cropped up since he'd marked the way, then finally ended up on a smooth incline. He flicked the headlights on, and, as though a light had shone down from heaven, we were greeted by a very large two-story lake home.

"Nice," I complimented him.

He beamed. "It even has a finished basement."

Three stories, then.

"It's lovely, sir," McKenzie said. "Really beautiful."

"Always thought I might retire here someday. But then, Dolly would've never known where to find me, and that would've been a tragedy," he replied.

The Jeep pulled up next to us, and Dolly hopped out. She came around the side to bang on Moose's door. "Okay now, you psychopath. You get yourself out of that truck and give Caleb somethin' to ease the pain. I ain't askin'."

"Anything you say." Moose grabbed the duffel bag next to him and got out of the truck. Dolly followed worriedly behind him.

"And another thing," she scolded. "You need to fix your damn roads!"

McKenzie and I got out of the truck and followed them.

"If I do that, people will think they can come visit," he argued.

"I don't care about that! Look at him. He looks awful." She scowled at him.

Moose stuck his head in the back of the Jeep and frowned. "Gonna have to check his stitches once we get inside."

"Oh no you don't. He ain't goin' nowhere until you shoot him up with somethin'." Dolly shook her finger at him.

He held up his hands. "You're right. I'm doin' that right now." He rummaged in his bag, got out the morphine kit that I recognized, and injected Caleb.

Shortly thereafter, Caleb relaxed.

"Okay. Shep. Will. Let's get him in the house," Moose said. "There's two rooms down the hall right off the kitchen. Put him in the one on the right."

I helped Shep lift Caleb, who still winced a bit, and carried him into the house once Moose opened the garage and let us in.

Just as Moose said, there was a hall off the kitchen that led to a pair of bedrooms. Jacey ran ahead of us to pull the covers back on the bed. Then Shep and I lowered Caleb down carefully onto the mattress on his stomach.

I could see already that there was blood seeping through his shirt. "Shit," I murmured.

"What?" McKenzie asked, poking her head in.

"Er—I'm sure it's nothing," I tried.

She stepped into the room and saw the blood. "*Nothing?!*"

"Nothing serious?" I amended with more hope than confidence.

As McKenzie glared at me, I could hear Moose rummaging in the kitchen.

"Got it," he finally cried triumphantly. "I knew I had another one stashed here."

"Moose, whatever it is you're gonna do, could you hurry it up?!" Dolly snapped.

"I'm just gonna stitch him back up. No need to panic," he said exasperatedly.

"You're takin' a tone with me again," Dolly warned.

"I ain't got no tone!" he replied.

Shep gave a rumbling laugh under his breath. "Just like old times."

FOURTEEN

MAKE-UP SEX

McKenzie

"Nothing serious?" I muttered to Will as Moose stitched up my father's back. There was still some blood but less and less as Dolly wiped it away while Moose was stitching.

"Well, nothing life-threatening, anyway," Will replied with a swallow. He was in deep shit, and he knew it.

I turned to face him. "What if it was me?"

"You?" he asked, confused.

"Yeah, me. With my stitches coming open and blood everywhere," I said.

His jaw clenched, and so did his hands. Then they relaxed. "It's not you. And your father's going to be fine. Moose said so."

"That's not the point, Will. You'd be losing your ever-loving mind, wouldn't you?" I accused, poking a finger in his chest.

He captured my hand. "Yes," he admitted. "I would be losing my ever-loving mind."

Mom knelt beside the bed, holding Dad's hand. I gestured to them. "This is my family. It's torture for all of us if one of us is hurt. You shouldn't make light of that."

"I wasn't trying to make light of it." He was hurt, I could hear it in his voice. "I just... didn't want you to worry."

"How was I not going to worry? My dad's back was bleeding!" I replied.

Mom sighed and looked at us. "Can you two take this someplace else? I don't want Caleb to have to worry about you two arguing."

"We're not arguing!" Will and I protested together.

"Your room's upstairs. The one with the yellow. You might want to use it," Moose said, not looking up from his work. "Your dad's gonna be fine.

I started to argue, but Will did something I never expected. He grabbed me and tossed me over his shoulder in a fireman's carry. "Will!"

"Sorry for any distress we might have caused. We'll go work this out," he apologized.

"You do that," Dolly said, glaring at me when I started to struggle.

Dad lifted his head a bit, frowning at Will.

I realized we really were distracting him. I stopped struggling and gave Dad a reassuring wave. "We're just going to go talk."

"For Christsake, do a lot more than that!" Dolly complained. "You gotta get the tension out. Don't come back down here until you can be civil to each other."

"We were just having a disagreement. We were perfectly civil!" I argued.

"Aaand on that note, we bid you goodnight." Will carried me away from my parents' bedroom and up the stairs just outside the living room.

"Goodnight? We're going back just as soon as we're done talking, mister!" I said, bouncing on his shoulder as we went upstairs.

"We're not." He poked his head into every bedroom until we reached the one on the right at the very end. It was dark outside but had four windows facing one direction, so I assumed our room must overlook the lake. "We're done for the night. We're upsetting everyone, and we're not going back to bother them anymore tonight. In fact, I might just get up and make them breakfast tomorrow as an apology." He set me down.

I sat down on the end of the bed, which was indeed covered by a yellow bedspread with tiny pink flowers on it. "You're supposed to be apologizing to me."

He frowned. "I just wanted you to feel better about the situation. Not to panic, you know? Moose would have said if he thought there was a real problem...."

"I'm not a baby. You don't have to handle me!" I snapped. "I can manage my own emotions. A hug and an 'I'm here' would have been just fine!"

Will sighed. "Fine, yes. I won't do it again."

I nodded, thinking that was it. But he just kept staring into the darkness beyond the windows. "Do you not see how it was the wrong thing to do?"

"I do." His answer was terse, and his body was tense.

"Are we fighting about something else I don't know about?" I hazarded.

He shook his head. "No." He went to the dresser and started opening drawers. "I'm hoping he's got some kind of sleepwear in here."

"For who?" I asked.

"For me. A T-shirt and a clean pair of boxers wouldn't be bad." He rummaged around in a drawer that held men's clothes, pulling out a black T-shirt and checking the size.

"Why would you need to wear anything?" I was getting more and more confused.

"You're going back downstairs, right? I figured I'd just turn in. I don't think you should go down, but I'm not going to stop you," he said.

That was certainly different from his earlier statement. "Look, just because I don't want you to treat me like a baby doesn't mean I don't value your opinion. If you think it's better that we stay up here, then we'll stay up here. I don't want to upset my parents any more than you do."

Will paused. "I'll find you a shirt. Here, you can have this one. It's not big enough for me." He handed me the black T-shirt.

I took it, reluctantly, and set it beside me on the bed. "Please tell me what's wrong."

"I don't want to talk about it right now." He went back to going through the different stacks of clothing.

I slid off the bed and put my hand on his shoulder. "Will?"

He stiffened under my touch. "McKenzie, let's just get ready for bed, okay?"

I considered it. On the one hand, I wanted to respect his boundaries, though there had never been a boundary like this between us before. On the other hand, I didn't want us going to bed mad. Option two won out. I wrapped my arms around his waist and pressed my cheek against his back. "Please, Will? Please?"

With a long, frustrated breath, he stopped rummaging and turned in my arms so we were facing each other. "Are we family, McKenzie?"

What kind of stupid question is that?! "What kind of stupid question is that?!" I blurted.

"It's not a stupid question. You were just saying how your parents are your family, and when one of you are hurt, it's torture for all of you." He looked me in the eye. "So I'm asking, are we family?"

"You're... upset because I called my parents family?" I blinked at him. Then it dawned on me. "And didn't include you."

"Now you're making me sound petty," he grumbled.

"No! No. It's not petty. It's not." I hugged him tightly. "Of course you're family. Under the best circumstances, you would have always been part of our family. I never meant to say you weren't." I stroked his cheek. "You're my someone."

Will was silent for a moment. Then, he embraced me properly, burying his face in my neck. "It's torture for me to see you in pain.

I'm sorry about before. I wasn't trying to 'handle' you. I just didn't know what I could say to make it better, and I had to try."

"I know. I know you had good intentions." I stroked his hair. "And I never meant to suggest you weren't family. I... can't even begin to tell you how important you are to me. I love you. I love you so much." The emotion was so powerful it brought tears to my eyes.

"I love you, too." His head came up, and he thumbed away my tears. "I didn't mean to make you cry," he said, even though his eyes were misty.

"I love you so much, I have to cry. There's no other way of dealing with emotions this big," I explained.

He cupped my face and kissed me. It was the tenderest kiss we'd ever shared.

When we broke apart, he did not go back to looking for clothes. In fact, as he held my eyes and deliberately began stripping off his shirt, I understood we were heading for a clothes-free event.

Thank God.

I wiggled out of the shorts and top I'd borrowed from Moose's farmhouse. By the time I'd done that, he was completely naked and hard. For me.

"You're still overdressed." He smiled, slipping his fingers under a bra strap and dragging it down, kissing my bare shoulder where it had been. He did the same with the other one.

My need pooled in my underwear and even my mouth watered. "Will?"

"Yes?" He deftly, yet slowly, undid the snap on the back of my bra.

"I think if we don't make love I'm going to die." I gasped as he slid my bra down my arms and tossed it aside. Cool air hit my breasts and my nipples perked up.

He smiled, looking right at them. "We can't have that, can we?" He palmed my breast.

I whimpered, pressing into his touch.

Will pressed soft kisses up my neck while taking both breasts in his hands and massaging my nipples. "Are you wet for me?" he asked hotly in my ear.

I nodded, not trusting myself to speak.

"Should I find out for myself?" he continued, beginning to gently pinch my nipples.

With a moan, I nodded again. The situation in my panties was getting worse by the second!

He stopped his attentions to my breasts but pulled me against him so our chests rubbed against each other when we breathed. His cock rubbed between us as well, and I trailed my fingertips up and down his shaft.

Will groaned. His hands shook as he hooked his fingers in the waistband of my panties and dragged them down as far as he could without our bodies losing contact.

In a dexterous move I was rather proud of, I got my panties the rest of the way to the floor and kicked them aside.

His hand pressed between my legs. "I'm a bad fiancé. Leaving you needing me for so long."

"I know a way you can apologize," I said, grinning at him.

He gave me a cheeky smile of his own then slid his fingers up inside me. "Oh? I'd love to hear it."

"Mm." I wasn't sure I was capable of coherent speech. "I... I want...."

"Go on. What do you want?" he asked, inserting a third finger as he rubbed my clit with his thumb.

"Ohmygod." I squeezed my eyes shut, fighting for sanity. "You. Please, Will, I want you."

His fingers withdrew, and I squeaked in indignation then squealed as he picked me up and deposited me on the bed.

"I love you, honeybee," he whispered against my lips. Then he widened my legs.

Desperate, I helped guide his dick into my entrance, keeping my knees splayed wide as I did so.

Will joined our bodies with one sure thrust.

I cried out, digging my nails into his skin. I knew he meant to be tender, but the second that huge cock of his was inside me, I was catapulted straight past tenderness.

And so was he.

"Fuck," he said, and, as his eyes squeezed shut, and a tremble of passion went through his entire body, I decided it was the highest compliment I'd ever been given.

I wrapped my legs around his waist, kissing the nail marks I'd already made on his shoulder. "Take me. Just like you want to."

He looked down at me. "Are you sure?" he panted.

I nodded.

Will kissed me hard and then began drilling me into the mattress.

I kissed him back, biting him a little.

He pulled back and pulled out, and I nearly screamed in protest. "What the—?!"

A strong finger touched my lips. "Don't worry," he said. "We're nowhere near finished."

"Then why—?"

Will pulled me up and turned me around, putting my hands around the bars of the wrought iron headboard behind us. "Hang on."

I swallowed. "Oh God."

"I think He'd approve." Then he grasped my hips and pulled back so I was bent nearly doggy style.

"Will?" I asked, looking at him over my shoulder.

He winked at me, then, still holding my hips in his tight grip, shoved in hard.

That was all it took. I came with a yell.

FIFTEEN

MISMATCHED FAMILY

Will

McKenzie clenched around my cock when she came. It was almost too much. But I'd be damned if I didn't see her all the way through her orgasm before having mine.

I kept thrusting, my hands tight on her hips. Because it was us, this was making love, but if it were any other couple, people would say they fucked like animals.

Truthfully, I didn't give a damn. All that mattered in all the universe were McKenzie and me.

She whimpered, clinging to the wrought iron bars on the headboard to keep from collapsing. I knew I was probably going too hard, but I couldn't help myself. The need was just too great.

When she came again, the delicious sensation around my cock had me seeing stars. It was instinct that had me pushing in as deep as I could go before I exploded inside her.

McKenzie slid down the bars and would have hit her head if I hadn't caught her. I drew us both back so she was sitting in my lap.

"You... are an animal... Will Masterson the Third," she panted.

She looked up at me while we both fought for breath. "A very... very bad man."

"I hope that's a compliment," I said cautiously.

"I haven't decided yet." She leaned her head back on my shoulder and closed her eyes. "That was *not* gentle."

"No," I conceded. "It wasn't."

"I'll bet you bruised my hips." She didn't sound angry about it. Just resigned.

I winced. "I wouldn't be surprised."

"Why are *you* flinching? *I'm* the one with the bruises," she muttered.

"Sorry. I never want to hurt you," I said contritely. I really did feel like an asshole.

"Then hold me like you mean it," she encouraged me.

I chuckled and the tension dissipated. I wrapped my arms around her, smoothing my hands over her soft skin. "Better?"

"Much." She closed her eyes. "Will?"

"Yes, honeybee?" I stroked my hands over her breasts.

"Oh my God, you want to go again already?!" She stared at me, incredulous.

I grinned. "When I'm with you? Always."

"Who else would you be with?" she snorted.

"Hm. Good point. I guess the answer is just 'always,'" I laughed. I slid one hand down to tease her intimately.

McKenzie moaned. "And here I was going to ask if we could sleep a little before another round."

"Sleep? Do you really want to sleep right now?" I asked, rolling her clit between my fingers.

"No." She arched against me. "Do it again, Will."

"Do what?" I asked, wondering which particular thing we'd just done she'd enjoyed so much.

"Me," she answered. "Do me."

I grinned. "Happily."

WE MADE LOVE UNTIL DAWN.

In the morning light, I saw that I did, indeed, leave finger bruises on McKenzie's hips. I resolved to be more careful in the future, even though she didn't seem bothered by them.

"Stop looking," she said once we stepped into the shower.

"Looking? At what?" I asked, starting to rinse her hair.

When her head came back from under the spray, she replied, "At my hips."

"Why?" I said, trying to make light of it. "They're perfectly nice birthing hips."

"Oh my God, you did not just say that." She rolled her eyes. "And that's not why you're looking at them, anyway. I had fun. You had fun. A good time was had by all. You don't need to worry about a few little bruises."

A few little bruises? I looked down at her hips. It was as though I'd been fingerprinted at the police station, but instead of using paper, they'd used her hips. "I'm not sure I'd call it a few little bruises...."

"I do, and mine's the only opinion that counts." She stroked my cheek then kissed me. "So you just deal with that."

I sighed and kissed her back. "All right. You win."

"As I always should," she teased me.

I laughed. I couldn't help myself.

McKenzie took the soap and started washing me. I grabbed some and did the same to her. Soon we were all soapy suds, hot water, and steam. And very turned on.

"Nope," she said, telling herself as much as me. "We have to go make breakfast. And see Dad. Though, if he's lucky, he's not awake yet."

I wondered just how many times over the course of my life I was going to be sporting blue balls because of this woman. But she was right. There were more important things right now.

Giving her a chaste kiss that telegraphed my understanding, I washed her off as non-sensually as I could. She did the same to me.

I washed and rinsed her hair, and mine, and then we got out and prepared for the day.

When we got downstairs, even though it was just past dawn, Dolly was already in the kitchen. We stopped short. "Um..." I murmured, trying not to wake the house.

"What?" Dolly asked.

"We were going to make breakfast for everyone," I said.

Dolly shook her head. "Not with my groceries, you weren't. I don't trust rich folks with the griddle."

I frowned. "I'm not that bad. And McKenzie is with me. She grew up on a farm."

"Then she can make the toast," Dolly said. "You go make sure Shep's outta bed. He's probably off for his walk, but you never know. Someone was makin' a lot of noise last night."

Heat crept up my neck. "Yes... well...."

McKenzie patted my arm. "Go find Shep. Where's Moose?"

Dolly inclined her head at the closed door to Caleb and Jacey's room. "He's givin' Caleb a look over and givin' him some more meds."

"Can we see him?" McKenzie asked. "Dad, I mean?"

"We're kinda hopin' he'll go back to sleep," Dolly said. "But we'll see what happens. Now, you, toast. You, Shep."

I nodded, kissed McKenzie's cheek, and went back upstairs to see if Shep was around. It didn't take much to figure out which bedroom was his. His clothes for the day were laid out on his bed.

Deciding he'd gone out in running gear or something, I went back downstairs and out the front door.

"Shep?" I called. I noted there were several trails leading off from the house. *Jesus, how am I ever going to find him?* I walked down the stairs of the wraparound decking. "Shep?" I yelled, standing in the yard. "Breakfast!"

There was no answer.

How far back do these paths go? I wondered where to start.

The crunch of leaves made me turn to the third path. There was Shep, leaning against a tree, winded.

"Shep, Jesus. You scared me. Dolly's saying it's time for breakfast soon.... Are you okay?" I asked as he hunched over.

"Get out," he wheezed, holding his middle.

"What?" I said, not understanding.

"They're... here. Get Mom. Get out." Then he collapsed.

I knew I should have heeded his warning, but it was Shep, and he was our friend. I couldn't abandon him. I ran to his side and rolled him onto his back. It was only then I saw the blood soaking through his black T-shirt.

"Moose!" I screamed, hauling Shep up. I needed to get him back to the safety of the house. "Moose!"

"That's 'sir' to y—shit." Moose stood out on the deck, staring as I half-dragged, half-carried Shep up the stairs. Moose shook himself and opened the door. "Get him inside."

I brought Shep into the house and laid him on the sofa Moose indicated in the living room. Dolly stopped what she was doing and ran out of the kitchen.

"What is it?" she gasped. "What's happened to my baby?!"

"He said they're here, and we need to get out," I said quickly. "Just before he collapsed."

Moose scowled. "Those motherfuckers." He tore open Shep's shirt. "He's been shot. Will, get my kit."

McKenzie beat me to it, scrambling into her parents' bedroom and coming out with the black case that held Moose's tools. She set it next to Moose and stood back.

I tucked her into my side.

"Now, Will, I'm gonna need you to be a man," Moose said calmly while he tried to stop the bleeding.

"Anything, sir," I replied.

Dolly was standing with her hands over her mouth, watching in horror as Moose worked vigorously to save her son.

"I need you to take McKenzie, Jacey, Dolly, and the other truck that's in the garage. The only thing I can think of is they were able to plant trackers on the truck and the Jeep at some point. I need you to take them, and the truck, and get outta here," Moose ordered.

"What about Dad and Shep?" McKenzie asked.

"They'll be stayin' here with me." Moose gave Dolly a significant look.

I knew what the look meant. "Shep's not going to make it, is he?"

"Not without some damn quick surgery. This is beyond my trainin'." Moose sighed. "No, he ain't gonna make it unless I give us up. I'm gonna try that. But you four ain't gonna be here when it happens. Now get goin'!"

"No, Shep! I can't just leave him!" Dolly protested.

Moose took her hand. "You're gonna have to. These other three need somebody with 'em with some survival skills."

"But—" Dolly said.

"You need to *go*, Dolly!" Moose ordered.

Dolly looked as though she might get defensive, then her shoulders drooped, and she nodded. "Take good care of him."

"Always," Moose said. He glared at me. "You plannin' on just standin' there?"

"No. We're leaving." I shooed Dolly and McKenzie toward the garage, stopping only to stick my head into Caleb and Jacey's room.

"I'm not leaving him," Jacey said, clearly having heard the conversation in the living room.

"Every second you waste, Shep loses more blood," I told her harshly. Moose was right. We didn't have time for any of this.

Jacey reeled back as though I'd slapped her. "You can leave without me—"

"Mother! Get in the *fucking* truck!" McKenzie surprised us all by shrieking.

"Go," Caleb said tiredly from the bed. "Just go. Please. For me."

Tears streaming down her cheeks, Jacey nodded, kissed Caleb's temple, and hurried out.

We made it to the truck, and I grabbed the keys and opened the garage door. Moose, ever prepared, had moved the Jeep behind the truck we'd driven to get here, leaving a space wide open for the blue truck we were using now.

As we got into the truck and I put it in gear, the air began to fill with smoke.

I wondered, briefly, if Moose had set the house on fire and was planning on taking the three of them down with the ship. But no, it was tear gas from the direction of the woods.

I put the truck in gear and peeled out of the garage. Men in tactical gear approached.

"Run them down," Dolly said without remorse.

I hit the 4-wheel drive and smashed right into the first one, going over him like a speed bump. I didn't know if he was the one who shot Shep, but I hoped he was. In fact, I was going to treat every damn one of them as though they did it.

When it became clear I had no intention of stopping, the mercenaries began shooting at the truck. Tires. Engine.

But whatever Moose had done to it rendered the bullets basically useless.

"He would have an armored truck," Dolly muttered. She was pale, afraid. We all were. Not of the mercenaries but for our loved ones.

"Do you think one of them managed to get a tracking device on the truck?" McKenzie asked when the mercenaries stopped shooting.

I swore under my breath, trying to concentrate on the hole-pocked drive out of the woods but now worried about tracking devices. "Fuck. I hope not."

"We'll switch cars quick. Once we've left them in the dust," Dolly said.

"Won't they just follow us?" Jacey asked. "I mean, they must have vehicles parked out on the road."

It was becoming clear to me that my grandfather had us trapped. Again.

As though the universe heard my thought, the end of the driveway leading out to the road was blocked by not one, but four law enforcement vehicles.

"Shit." I looked behind us, wondering if there was anywhere to go if I threw the truck in reverse.

"Will," I heard over a loudspeaker. "Don't be an idiot. Get out of the truck and get your friends some medical attention. Milton didn't look good."

"Ike." I stared out the windshield at the man himself, arm in a sling, smiling triumphantly at us. I looked at Dolly. "What should I do?"

She stared at the same situation we were. "Give him what he wants."

SIXTEEN

WHAT HE WANTS

McKenzie

Will stepped out of the truck with his hands over his head.

"That's great, Will, but I think there are three lovely ladies still in the truck," Ike said.

Mom, Dolly, and I looked at each other then got out as well, hands raised.

"Excellent. See how easy things can be when you cooperate, Will?" Ike asked. "Though I do keep having to hammer that lesson home over and over again. Your grades in college do not suggest that you're a slow learner but...."

"You've got us. Now, get Shep help," Will said.

Ike tapped his chin, stalling.

"*IKE!!!*" Will snarled.

"Fine, fine. A deal's a deal." Ike turned to Horacio, who was hovering nearby. "Send in a medical team."

Horacio got on his phone immediately.

"Now. Will, ladies. Would you mind following me to that Escalade over there?" Ike asked sweetly.

Another black car.

I laughed. I couldn't help it. I laughed hysterically. I had to hold my sides, it hurt so badly, but I couldn't stop.

Ike sighed. "Will, fix it."

Will lowered his arms and went straight to my side, putting his arms around me. "Hey, love. It's going to be okay."

"We don't lie to each other." I hiccuped between giggles.

"I'm going to make it okay." He sounded very determined. Sure of himself.

That made my laughter turn to tears. "Everyone around us just gets hurt."

Ike rolled his eyes. "Tick-tock, Will."

"Let's talk about it in the car," Will said kindly. He started walking me that way. "Come on."

Mom and Dolly followed behind.

I felt like a complete idiot, but I couldn't stop crying. And laughing. And crying. "I'm s-sorry," I sobbed at them once we were situated in the back of the Escalade.

"It's all right." He rocked me gently and kissed my hair. "It's all been very upsetting. It's only natural to fall apart sometimes."

Panic set in once the door swung closed. Ike and Horacio got in front, Horacio in the driver's seat.

"They're never going to let us go," I whispered. I jumped to my door and began tearing at the handle, clawing at it. But the child locks were on.

I couldn't breathe. I needed to get out.

"McKenzie. McKenzie!" Will grabbed me and held my arms against my sides. "You're hurting yourself!"

I fought him, screaming, "Let go of me! Let go!"

Mom crawled across the back seat. "McKenzie, you need to calm down." She took my hands in hers.

I felt a sting and looked down. My hands were bleeding at the tips, and my nails were ragged. The blood brought me down rapidly.

Ike, the asshole, laughed from the front seat. "Let's go, Horacio. They have it handled."

Horacio pulled off the side of the road and started toward the highway. I noticed a black sedan pull out in front of us and one behind.

They weren't taking any chances.

I hiccuped again and leaned into Will. Now that I was calm, I was exhausted. Just exhausted from all of it.

Will pulled me into his lap. "You're okay, honeybee."

Mom went back to Dolly, who was looking fierce, but pale. I knew she must be terrified about Shep.

"Ike, you have to keep us updated on Shep's condition," Will said as though reading my mind.

"Horacio will keep an eye on his texts. Won't you, Horacio?" Ike replied.

Horacio just nodded.

"He's driving," Will pointed out.

"Phone mount. What century are you living in?" Ike chuckled.

Will frowned.

"In my century, everyone's supposed to be buckled up. But I'm willing to overlook it today," Ike added.

"How magnanimous of you," Will responded bitterly.

I slipped my arms around Will at the very suggestion we might have to be parted, even if it would be just for safety's sake. I didn't want to sit even an inch away from him. Not now.

We fell into silence for twenty minutes.

Finally, Dolly couldn't take it anymore. "Have they called an ambulance?" she demanded.

"We sent in the medical team. *Our* medical team. It has a surgeon on it," Ike said. "If your son has a chance, that team will make sure he's stable and get him to... a facility."

"One of Grandfather's facilities," Will inferred.

"With a medical staff. I think Caleb and Milton will do very well there," Ike assured him. "Provided Milton survives."

"He prefers Shep," I mumbled.

"I'm sure he does." Ike settled back in his chair.

Will growled. "There has to be *some* news by now!"

"Ugh. You are so needy." Ike looked at Horacio. "Well?"

"They're still working. Lieutenant Stanley Isaacs was apprehended. What do you want us to do with him?" Horacio asked.

"Moose?" I mouthed to Dolly.

Dolly nodded.

"Take him to the facility as well. We don't kill our friends, now do we, Will?" Ike said.

It was a threat.

"No. We don't," Will replied.

"Good man. Getting smarter. You might become worthy of your grandfather's empire yet!" Ike chortled.

"Joy," Will grumbled under his breath.

Ike snickered. "I swear it has been the highlight of my life educating you. I've never had this much fun!"

"I'm glad someone is." Will didn't look resigned. He looked angry.

The fact that he still had spirit left in him after all this gave me hope. I threaded my fingers through his.

"Now, when we get back, there will be the engagement party. Caleb, sadly, does not appear to be in fit condition to attend. We'll just have to rely on Jacey. We've moved the party, of course, from Bran's home to that of John Anders. He's such a good friend of your grandfather's and was happy to help," Ike said.

"What day?" I asked.

"Tomorrow, of course. It is very fortuitous that we found you in time. Poor John has been making so many preparations," Ike responded.

"Tomorrow?!" Will gaped.

Ike turned back again. "I thought it best to move up the timeline a bit."

"Tomorrow didn't seem a bit early to you?" Will argued.

"Not in the slightest. You two have proven to be quite vexing. Entertaining, but vexing. I'm going to make it so that there is nowhere you can go where you won't be recognized." Ike's tone became flat, menacing.

"So, a well-publicized engagement," I said.

Ike smiled at me and it gave me the creeps. "Exactly. We've gone all out. This will be the engagement event of the century!"

"I see." Will rubbed the back of my neck. He must have felt my tension. "I guess you think you have us trapped."

"Pretty sure I do this time. But you're always welcome to try again. It's truly exhilarating chasing you," Ike chuckled.

"I'm going to make you hate me, Ike," Will said.

Ike just laughed harder. "Oh, Will. I already do."

"He's stable enough to transport," Horacio interrupted.

"Hm? Oh, good. Not out of the woods, but not dead, I'm assuming," Ike replied.

Dolly let out a long breath. It was then that I saw she was gripping Mom's hand.

"Yes, that is correct, sir," Horacio said.

"That's good news." Ike scrolled through his phone. "I hope you like truffles."

"Truffles?" I echoed. "What does that have to do with Shep?"

Ike shook his head. "No, your engagement party. They will be serving truffles."

"Ike, respectfully, do you think we give a flying fuck about truffles right now?" Will hissed.

"Caviar, then?" Ike replied cheekily.

"When can we see Dad, Shep, and Moose?" I asked, ignoring the engagement party talk.

"You really are poo-pooing all the hard work John and I put into this." Ike sighed. "And I think it would be best if you weren't allowed to see them until after the party. No offense, but you do have a history of making trouble, and I thought a little incentive might be in order." Then he chuckled. "The man actually calls himself 'Moose'? Where do you pick up these people?"

"Are you making fun of my Moose?" Dolly asked angrily. "While my son might be dying?"

Ike raised an eyebrow at her. "Yes, I think I am. And if I'm very, very lucky, he will die. One less persistent problem I have to deal with."

"You sonofabitch!" Dolly began crawling over the seat to get to Ike.

Mom grabbed her by the waistband of her pants while Will and I gripped her shoulders. "No, Dolly! This is what he wants!" Will cried.

Indeed, I could see the barrel of a gun poking out from under Horacio's jacket, even as he placidly pretended to just drive.

"Come on, Dolly. Don't you want to punish the man responsible for hurting your son?" Ike goaded her.

Dolly let out a scream of frustration and scratched Will's cheek.

"Hey now. None of that. He has to look presentable tomorrow!" Ike objected.

"Leave her alone!" I yelled at Ike. "Dolly, please. Look at me. Horacio has a gun. He's going to shoot you if you get any closer. What will Shep do without his mom?"

Dolly took several deep breaths then let Mom drag her back by her pants. She shook with rage, but she wasn't wild-eyed anymore.

Ike clucked his tongue. "Well, that was disappointing."

"If you want me to be good, you're going to have to keep everyone I love alive," Will said coldly.

Ike gave a disgruntled huff. "No guarantees on Shep."

"I want to make sure every effort is made for him," Will pressed on.

"Ugh. Fine. You are *such* a pain in the ass." Ike reached in his pocket then handed Will a handkerchief. "You're bleeding."

"Whose fault is that?" Will pressed the handkerchief to his cheek.

"It figures Masterson would put someone even crazier than he is in charge of his operations while he's in prison," Mom said.

Ike grinned. "Thank you. That's high praise coming from you."

Mom grumbled that it wasn't a compliment, but Ike was still happy.

"So, back to the engagement event. Or maybe we should call it an extravaganza. There will be three chocolate fountains, a very large champagne fountain, six ice sculptures, five four-tiered cakes and one eight-tiered one, and fireworks, of course. We've also got six swans to paddle around John's pond—he had two but more is more—and we've got seven five-star Michelin restaurants catering. There will be dancing, of course. There will be too many gifts to do a gift opening right there. Let's just say you will be writing thank-you cards for a while, McKenzie." Ike looked very proud of himself. "Oh, and Jacey, as mother of the bride-to-be, you will, of course, be required to be circulating and social as well."

"Of course," Mom said quietly, her arms around Dolly.

"What will Dolly be doing?" I asked.

"Whatever she wants. At the estate. She won't be attending. It's bad enough we have two hayseeds in attendance. I still don't know what your grandfather is thinking." Ike shrugged. "But that's above my pay grade, I'm afraid."

"If you could bring yourself to stop insulting my future wife, I'd be greatly appreciative," Will grunted.

Ike chuckled. "I'll work on that."

"Sir?" Horacio said.

"Yes?" Ike replied.

"They're at the facility. Mr. Pope is being taken into emergency surgery. It's touch and go, I guess." Horacio gestured to his phone. "I guess they moved him too soon."

Ike waved a hand. "They needed to get him out of there regardless."

Dolly made a strangled sound.

"Also, Mr. Killeen attacked one of the guards," Horacio said.

"What?!" Ike grabbed Horacio's phone off the mount. "How?! *How* could that even happen?!"

"The guard reacted, sir," Horacio went on, even as Ike was reading it for himself.

"Fuck. *FUCK.*" Ike slammed the phone back into the mount and closed his eyes.

Mom leaned forward. "What do you mean, the guard 'reacted'?" Her voice was tight with fear.

My stomach was in hard knots. I clutched Will's shirt, afraid of the next words out of Ike's mouth.

"Caleb took a bullet to the heart. He's in surgery, but he's not expected to live. Fuck, Mr. Masterson is going to kill me! We broke one of his favorite toys," Ike complained.

Mom turned absolutely transparent. "Caleb," she whispered.

Then she passed out in Dolly's arms.

SEVENTEEN

NOT GOOD ALL AROUND

Will

The estate was just as we'd left it. Large. Full of every amenity one could think of.

Oppressive.

It was a prison. It might have a pool, a chef, and even its own tennis court, but it was a prison nonetheless.

Dolly and McKenzie got the still-woozy Jacey out of the Escalade. Horacio took his gun out and pointed it at us, gesturing for us to go into our gilded cage.

"What's the latest on Caleb and Shep?" I asked, going over to the women and offering my arms.

Jacey stumbled, and I caught her. By silent agreement between Dolly, McKenzie, and I, I scooped the woman who'd given birth to me up in my arms and began carrying her into the mansion.

"Milton is out of surgery. It's touch and go for now. They're still working on Caleb," Ike said.

Dolly gave a relieved sigh. "As long as he's out of surgery, my Shep'll make it."

"We'll see. I'm hoping for a Hail Mary from the universe for

Caleb. Mr. Masterson will be *so* angry if he dies." Ike bemoaned his situation.

"Maybe we'll get really lucky, and he'll kill you," I said darkly, walking through the front door with a sense of dread.

"Now, Will. No need to be petty," he replied with a sniff. He followed us in, Horacio pulling up the rear, keeping his gun trained on the four of us. Not on Ike, of course. But McKenzie, Dolly, Jacey, and me, we were all in danger.

Dolly gave a low whistle. "Too bad your granddad's such an asshole. This looks like it could be a nice place to live."

"It's a bit lonely, but yes. It's got all the furnishings," I said.

"Well, it won't be lonely anymore. You've got company." Ike grinned.

"All things being equal, I wish they were free, and I was here alone," I muttered.

McKenzie waited until I put Jacey down in a lounger out on the patio before swatting my arm. "We talked about this!"

"I know. And I'm always going to wish I could have kept you safe," I said quietly.

"It's so delicious seeing you taken down to the level where you belong," Ike crowed. "I swear, seeing you so humbled is my favorite dessert."

"Did you *ever* have a soul?!" McKenzie snapped.

Ike pretended to think about it. "No, can't say that I did. A soul doesn't keep me in the lifestyle to which I've become accustomed." He sat down in a patio chair.

Horacio waved his gun, and we all took seats.

"Now, Jacey, I'm going to need you to get it together by tomorrow," Ike said pleasantly. "Even, and especially, if he dies. I'm sure you are worried about Dolly and Shep's wellbeing as well. Not to mention McKenzie's. Mr. Masterson is only so indulgent. Ask Will."

I ground my teeth but didn't rise to the bait.

Jacey just stared at him. "You're unbelievable," she whispered.

"So I'm told." He smirked. "Be that as it may, I do need you to be the smiling, doting mother tomorrow. Whatever happens is Caleb's own fault for being terminally stupid. Life goes marching on."

"I think we get the point, Ike," I said angrily. "There's no need to be cruel."

"I know. I just enjoy it. You have been a real pain in the ass. All of you have." He gestured to his wounded arm.

"Boo-hoo," Dolly snarked.

Ike scowled at her. "When Mr. Masterson gets tired of you, you're going to be 'disappeared' first."

"I'd like to see you try," she shot back.

"And we can let this one go for now. We get the point. Everyone's pissed off at everyone else. We need to be on our best behavior tomorrow. Yes, fine. We'll be perfect. The perfect couple. The perfect family. You make sure Shep and Caleb get the best possible care," I said.

"I am. Your grandfather just didn't have the heart to kill them all, since they're such good friends of yours," Ike sighed. "Pity."

"Before I meet my maker, I'm sending you to hell." Dolly snarled.

McKenzie put a hand on her shoulder. "Please, Dolly. Let it go for now."

Dolly's jaw worked. She glared death at Ike. But she finally agreed. "For now."

"Great," Ike said. "Now that we all know what the score is, I think we can get you all settled. Polly?"

The housekeeper came out of the shadows. "Yes, Mr. Freeborn?"

"Please make sure Miss Pringle and Mrs. Killeen are given comfortable accommodations. They've had a difficult day." He smiled at Polly.

She nodded. "Yes, sir. Two guest rooms have been made up per your earlier request."

"Perfect. I knew I could count on you." He turned back to us. "All right. Off you go."

I stood and took McKenzie's hand. She turned to her mother. "Mom, are you going to be okay?"

"I'll get her where she's goin'. She needs to rest," Dolly said, gently taking Jacey's arm and pulling her out of the lounger. She paused. "How we gonna find out how Shep and Caleb are doing?"

"Ah, yes." Ike reached into his pocket...

... And handed me a cell phone.

"What?" I asked, confused.

"Don't get excited. There are only a few numbers that are allowed to dial or text out or in. I figured I've got you by the balls, so I don't need to worry about you having one of these. Plus, your grand-father would like to talk to you. Soon. I'd suggest when the prison comes up on caller ID, you answer," he said.

I stared at the phone for a moment. Then I shook myself. "Are you going to keep me updated?"

"Horacio or I will keep you abreast of the situation, yes. Oh!" He rattled off a six-digit passcode. "Memorize that."

"It's my birthday," I replied.

"Then you won't forget it, will you?" He rolled his neck and straightened his jacket with one hand. "All right, Horacio. I think we're done here. Polly will let you know the details about the engage-ment party. Make your grandfather proud!"

"Wouldn't dream of doing anything else," I muttered.

He nodded and stalked off, taking Horacio with him.

"Are you ready to be shown to your rooms?" Polly asked politely.

Dolly looked at her as though she'd sprouted a third arm. "You know we're bein' held prisoner here, right?"

"Yes. Are you ready to see your rooms?" Polly asked again, completely unfazed.

Dolly shook her head slowly. "Will, I gotta say, you're surrounded by the most horrible people I've ever had the misfortune to meet. I don't know why you didn't run off sooner."

"Habit," I admitted. "Polly, we'll come along. We need to see which rooms they're in so I can keep them apprised of things."

"They are in the rooms directly across the hall from you, sir," she responded with a shrug. "You may retire as well for an afternoon rest.

I imagine you have not eaten in a while. I will bring you something from the kitchen."

I considered arguing that we could all sit out on the patio to eat. That way, we wouldn't be apart. However, looking at Jacey, Dolly, and McKenzie, I realized we'd all been through the wringer and needed some down time. "All right."

"Excellent. Follow me, please." She led us all to the wing where McKenzie and my room was, and, sure enough, opened one of the doors directly across the hall. "Miss Pringle, this is your room. Please use the intercom on the wall if you need anything. Most unfortunately, I am to lock you in your room. Mr. Freeborn thinks you might cause trouble, regardless of your son's condition."

"I would never do anything that would hurt my son," Dolly objected.

"I'm sorry. Mr. Freeborn's orders were clear. I will come with something to eat shortly," Polly said.

Dolly turned to me. "I don't suppose you get a say in this."

I sighed and raked a hand through my hair. "Not even a tiny one."

"Figures. I'm gonna give your grandfather a punch in the nose one of these days." She stomped into the room and slammed the door shut.

True to her word, Polly locked her in.

Jacey went shakily into her room. I let go of McKenzie's hand to go lift her mother into bed. "If anyone can survive what happened, it's Caleb," I assured her.

"Yes. I am told he is very hard to kill," Polly chimed in.

"No one asked you." McKenzie hissed at her.

Polly shrugged. "I'm simply stating facts."

"Caleb will be fine," Jacey said, her voice only trembling slightly. "He always is. He wouldn't leave me."

I nodded. "I believe that."

She suddenly gripped my hand. "Promise me you'll tell me right away if there's any news. *Any* news. E-either way."

I squeezed her hand between both of mine. "I promise."

Jacey nodded and laid back against the pillows. "I don't know if I'll be able to sleep, but Caleb will want me strong. So, I'm going to try."

"We'll watch the phone around the clock, Mom," McKenzie said.

"I know you will, my darling girl." Jacey closed her eyes.

McKenzie smoothed back her mother's hair and kissed her forehead. "It'll be okay, Mom. We're going to make it okay."

Jacey smiled sadly. "We used to say that, too."

Eyes shimmering, McKenzie turned to me. "Will?"

I wrapped her in my arms then guided her across the hall to our room. I saw Polly lock Jacey in and was not the least bit surprised when a skeleton key turned in our lock as well once the bedroom door was closed.

"I guess we're all troublemakers." McKenzie sniffled, trying to smile.

I held her more tightly and kissed her hair. "You can cry, honeybee. There's no one here but you and me."

"And assorted cameras." She choked back a sob. "I don't want to give them the satisfaction."

"Okay. I understand." I rubbed her back, trying to comfort her.

"Will?" she said softly after a while.

I'd been wondering where Polly was with our food, but my attention snapped right back to McKenzie. "Yes, honeybee?"

"Make love to me?" she asked. "Make me feel good?"

I looked into her tear-filled eyes. My heart broke. There wasn't a lot I could do for her, but I could do that. I leaned down and kissed her. "Of course, honeybee."

EIGHTEEN

BUTTERFLIES

McKenzie

Will kissed me again, stroking his tongue against mine. In one motion, he pushed down my shorts and panties, pushing up my shirt to brush his lips over my belly. I gasped as he kissed lower.

"A-are you—!" I gasped, wondering why we weren't going to the bed.

"Hang on," he murmured, latching onto my core.

I'd have stumbled if I wasn't so worried about hurting Will. He said to hang on, but I wasn't sure what to hang on *to*! I gripped his hair as his tongue did sinful things to my body, my other hand on his shoulder to keep me upright.

"Will," I panted as he sucked on my clit. "I-I'm going to fall over soon! I don't want to break your neck!"

He chuckled against me, and that added a whole new sensation. Just before I would have come and probably put him in the hospital, he stopped and popped his head out. "Are you that worried, honeybee?"

"Y-yes!" My teeth were chattering.

"Okay. I think I need to give you something else, anyway. Much as I love it when you come around my tongue, I like it when you come around my cock better," he said hotly.

Those words alone could have finished me off except that he was already lifting me. I flopped on the bed, legs splayed wide, desperate for what he was going to give me.

"God I wish we were both naked, but I can't wait," he murmured, his tone strained. He opened his pants, got on top of me, and pushed right in.

I arched my back, coming with a cry as he filled me.

Will groaned. "Yes-s-s-s, that's it." He threaded his fingers through mine, his other hand pushing up under my T-shirt and bra to squeeze my breast as he started to thrust.

They were sharp and deep, and I whimpered. I was still loose enough from the last time we made love, but for some reason, every time we did it, it was still so overwhelming!

"Deep breaths, honeybee. We're going to be at this for a while," he cooed.

"Oh God," I moaned, knowing full well what that meant. We weren't going to be finished until I passed out from pleasure.

"He can't help you now," he rumbled. Even his voice had become gravelly and sinful.

I was sure he was right. And why would God want to? He knew what was good for me.

Fucking Will was very, very good for me.

As I'd hoped, all thoughts about our situation, Dolly, Mom, Shep, and even Dad melted from my mind with the heat of our lovemaking. I squeezed Will's hand and moved with him, my arm draped around his neck so I could hold on for dear life.

He kissed me and tweaked my nipple while moving relentlessly inside me. My orgasm flooded me, coming on unexpectedly, and I shrieked, digging my nails into the back of his neck as I came apart around him.

Will grunted, and I felt his hot seed deep inside me as he came as well. But he didn't lose his hard on, and, after the last drops of his release, he began thrusting again.

"I-I d-don't know if I c-can—" I said, my voice trembling.

"Does honeybee want to try a different position?" he asked softly.

That wasn't exactly what I was trying to say. And it was going to be problematic, anyway. "I c-can't ride you r-right now. T-too much!"

He chuckled, and then I was on my side, bracing myself on the mattress. Behind me, he raised my leg and kissed his way down my skin before putting my leg over his shoulder. "Let's try this, honeybee."

Will entered me again from behind, his hand firmly planted on my hip as he began fucking me hard. But he didn't go as deep, which might have been the point of the position.

Still, I didn't like this as much as when I was facing him, and, though I was definitely going to reach climax again soon, I pouted a little.

"Aw, is my honeybee not happy?" he asked, concerned.

I turned my head so I could kiss him. "I like it better when we're facing each other."

"Ah. I see." He pulled out.

I thought the loss might kill me. "Will!"

"Shh. I'm just doing what you asked." Then, I was underneath him again.

I wasn't letting him move me around anymore until I got my orgasm. I locked my legs around his waist while he pushed his big, thick dick back inside me.

He laughed and stroked the hair off my face. "Greedy much?"

"Very," I growled back. "Now, fuck me Will Masterson the Third!"

"Bossy. I like it." He grinned at me then began drilling me like a jackhammer.

It was fantastic. I clung to him, raising my hips to meet his thrusts as we coupled desperately. Both of us seemed to want to keep the rest of the world at bay.

This time when I came, I felt *and* saw fireworks. I moaned underneath him as he hammered me all the way through my orgasm. Then he came, hot, inside me again.

"I don't think... I can..." I said breathlessly.

He kissed me. "Just lay still. I'll do all the work. I need at least one more round. Is that okay, honeybee?"

How does he have this much stamina?! I looked at his hopeful expression and sighed, tapping my forehead to his. "If I pass out, you keep going until you finish."

Will smiled widely and kissed me. "Thank you, honeybee."

"The things I do for love," I jokingly lamented.

He laughed and had just begun thrusting again when the phone Ike had given him dinged on the bedside table.

We were both catapulted back to reality. Will reached across to grab the phone and stared at the screen.

"How-how's Dad?" I asked, my voice tight with fear.

He sagged with relief. "He made it out of surgery fine. He's recuperating. They're optimistic."

I wriggled, trying to get to the phone to see for myself.

Will gently pulled out and scooted me up next to him, handing me the phone.

I read the screen two, three, four times. Then, what I'd been hoping wouldn't happen while they were recording us happened.

I burst into tears.

He wrapped me in his arms. "It's okay, honeybee. It's all looking good." He paused. "We need to tell your mother."

"I wish they'd said something about Shep," I whispered.

As though they'd heard me—and they might have—another text came through.

Will and I read it together.

"Shep's almost out of the woods, too." He looked at our locked bedroom door. "Maybe they'll hear me if I yell...."

"It's all right, sir. I've already told them." Polly's voice came over the intercom. "I can come in with your food any time. I didn't want to bother you while you were... otherwise engaged."

I could hear him grind his teeth. "Thank you, Polly. I think we will have our food now."

"Of course, sir. Would you like me to wait until you get dressed?" she asked politely.

"Doesn't seem like there's much of a point. Just bring it on a tray and set it on the bed," he sighed.

"Yes, sir." The com closed, and, within minutes, Polly was at our door.

For some reason, she still knocked before coming in. "I've brought you braised salmon with asparagus and new potatoes with a white wine pairing."

"And water?" Will asked. He had the duvet pulled up to his waist.

I had it over my chest.

"Oh, yes, of course, sir. Mr. Freeborn would be most unhappy if Miss Kent was too sick to attend the festivities tomorrow," she said.

"Good. Set it down, and you can leave," he replied coldly.

"Thank you, Polly," I added, though I'm not sure what compelled me.

She smiled and nodded, setting the tray down on the end of the bed.

Once she was gone, having locked the door behind her, I turned to Will. "Shouldn't we try to make her our friend?"

"Not really sure that'll work. But if you want to try, you're welcome to," he responded, sounding defeated. He pulled the tray up to us, and we balanced it on our thighs.

I forked up some salmon and offered it to him to eat. "Can't hurt to try, can it?"

He took a bite and chewed it thoughtfully. "I just hate the idea of cozying up to any of these bastards." He used his fork to feed me a potato.

It was the perfect texture with vibrant seasoning. If we weren't trapped in a hellscape of a paradise, I would have complimented the chef.

"Now, don't go making that face, or we'll never finish dinner before it gets cold," he murmured, stroking his fingertips down my arm.

I shivered. "What face?"

"The Will-I'm-about-to-come face," he said.

"What?" I cried, incredulous. "I would not make that face over a potato!"

"You would. Because you just did," he grinned.

I groaned. "Seriously?!"

"Seriously," he confirmed.

"Well... they are good potatoes," I mumbled.

Will laughed. "Fine. Let me try them."

"You won't be able to resist," I warned him.

"Try me." He opened his mouth.

I speared a potato and popped it in his mouth.

He chewed it slowly, both eyebrows rising in surprise. "This does taste good."

"See? *See?!*" I crowed.

"Not orgasmic, though," he teased.

I crossed my arms over my chest. "I was not about to have an orgasm over a potato."

"You were."

"It would at *least* had to have been chocolate cake," I sniffed.

We both looked down at the tray at a cloche. Will pulled it off. Sure enough, there was a huge slice of chocolate cake sitting in the corner, more than enough for both of us.

"I have an idea," he smiled mischievously.

"No, don't you even," I said, pretty sure I knew where his mind was going.

"I haven't even told you what it is yet," he said.

"You want to do something dirty with that cake," I accused.

Will popped a bite of salmon in my mouth. "Well, obviously."

"Mfph." I munched as quickly as possible so I could answer him, but it was hard. The salmon was also divine, and I wanted to savor it.

"The salmon, too? Really?" he teased.

I frowned at him and swallowed. "It's not my fault you have such a good chef on staff."

"He needs a raise if all I have to do is ply you with his food to get you in the mood." He looked down at the tray then set it aside.

"Hey!" I objected. "We're not done eating yet!"

"We're not," he agreed. He picked up the plate of chocolate cake and threw the duvet back so we were both uncovered. "It's time for dessert."

"Will! We do have to eat *actual* food every once in a while or we won't be able to keep having sex! We'll both be too spent." I thought I made a good point. I was also a bit afraid, if the salmon and potatoes had nearly done me in, as he said, then the chocolate cake might put me right over the edge.

That would be so embarrassing!

"I'll have Polly reheat it. It will give you an opportunity to butter her up. That's your plan, right?" He prowled down the bed and set the plate down just so he could grab my ankles and pull me down so I was flat on my back.

"You're not actually going to—" I gasped, glancing at him.

He picked up a piece of cake with his fingers and smeared it on my leg. "I absolutely am."

Then his tongue was on my skin.

Still sensitive all over from our last rounds, my whole body started to tingle. "I-is the cake good?" I asked, trying to distract myself.

"Very. But I know other things that taste better. I prefer honey to chocolate," he said, his voice deep and sexy.

I knew exactly what he was talking about, and my whole body flushed with desire and embarrassment. "Where are you planning to get honey?"

"You know where." He dipped his fingers inside me.

"Will!" I cried, gasping as my body clenched needily around his fingers.

"That's more like it. I don't like being one-upped by a potato," he said, adding a third finger while thumbing my clit.

I gripped the sheets. After our last session, I'd thought it would be impossible to bring my body to orgasm again, but once more, he proved me wrong.

He drew his hand back, much to my consternation, and licked his fingers. "That's where honey comes from."

"Will, for God's sake!" I begged, writhing on the bed.

With a grin, he took a glob of cake and frosting on his finger then moved up my body. "Suck," he said, his finger hovering over my mouth.

If that was all I needed to do to get him going, I was more than happy to do it. I wrapped my lips around his finger and licked it sensually.

He groaned, and, at the same time, thrust his cock into me all the way to the hilt.

The chocolate cake really was orgasmic. Or he was. Or both. In any case, I came, my body nearly levitating off the bed.

"And now I need to be jealous of chocolate cake," he grumbled good-naturedly. But then he kept going. And going. And going.

By the time I came for the last time, I'd completely forgotten any kind of cake existed, much less chocolate.

"Or maybe not," Will whispered in my ear as he filled me again.

NINETEEN

THE EVENT OF THE SEASON

Will

"... And then Cass said, 'It's just peanuts. Why would I care?'" Joel Westlake chortled, nearly spilling his drink on me as he gestured expansively with it.

I took a prudent step back. "Gee that's very... classist..." I muttered, knowing Joel was three sheets to the wind and wouldn't clock anything I was saying anyway.

"I know, right?!" He didn't stop laughing.

John Anders, our long-suffering host, came over then and took him by the shoulders. "Come on, Joel. Let's go get you some water."

Joel made a face. "Water? Who wants water?"

"You do. Trust me." John gave me an apologetic look then steered Joel away.

I looked over at McKenzie. She was wearing a pretty white sleeveless dress with tiny pink rosettes on it. Her beautiful honey hair fell loose around her shoulders.

All I wanted to do was find some nice, hidden nook and divest her of that dress, but currently she was sitting on white wrought iron lawn furniture surrounded by a gaggle of giggling girls.

She caught my eyes, and I could almost hear her mind screaming, *Help me!*

I smiled and started over.

A man in a white linen suit blocked my path.

I stumbled back. "I'm sorry, I...." I looked up and couldn't hold back a gasp. "Holy shit—"

Bran's livid red, scarred lips fought to smirk and failed. "I know I look like shit. Thanks to you."

"I would argue that it's thanks to you. What the fuck are you even doing here? I thought for sure you'd still be laid up," I said.

"I wouldn't have missed this for the world." He was pocked with swatches of gauze, other burns left to heal in the open air.

Freddy Krueger had nothing on him.

"I can't believe your vanity let you leave the house in your condition. Are you going to throw acid on me now, too?" I asked, trying to sound nonchalant.

"Oh no. I was thoroughly frisked before I came in, as was every other person here, including the staff. No, I came to watch you squirm," he said.

I raised an eyebrow. "I guess I would in the presence of a snake like you."

He chuckled. "No, that's not what I mean. I've decided I'm going to watch as you fall off your moral high horse and have your spirit crushed into dust. I will be at every meeting, every gathering, every party, every event. I'll even keep going to gallery openings just to see you crawl, beg, and lick your grandfather's boots. That will sustain me for the rest of my life, I think."

"I won't be licking anyone's boots," I stated coldly. "Now, if you'll excuse me...."

"She would have liked it. Once I pinned her down, and she stopped struggling, she would have enjoyed being with me," he said as I pushed past him.

I turned back, so furious I could barely see straight. Then, I looked at his ruined face. I gently tapped his cheek in a 'friendly' manner and he winced. "Sorry. I don't punch out the feeble and infirmed." I walked away.

Ike appeared beside me seconds later, another obstacle on my quest to get to McKenzie. "Your grandfather has requested your presence at the office on Monday. Since you were unable to make it last week, I would suggest being prompt."

"I would hate to upset Grandfather," I grumbled.

"I know you would. Because you know what happens to people who upset him." He gestured to Bran.

Bran waved.

A sick feeling unfurled in my stomach. "He would never do that to me."

"Don't be so sure. You've made him *quite* angry." He put an arm around me. "I had to remind him that Dolly and Milton's impromptu escape plan was never your idea and, in fact, completely unknown to you. You did still fight Horacio, but we've decided to chalk that up to McKenzie's influence. He's starting to dislike that whole family as well. Do you see where this is going?"

And there it was, me being slowly crushed to dust right before Bran's eyes. My jaw tightened, and I nodded. "I'll be good."

"What's that? I can't quite hear you," Ike prompted.

"I've never been so committed to being good in my entire life," I said more forcefully.

He smiled. "Good boy. Now, let's go get a drink."

"I was actually going to—" I pointed in McKenzie's direction.

Ike shook his head. "A drink. Now." His hand locked on my shoulder so I couldn't get away without causing a scene.

Bran followed us into the house then into a well-appointed study. It was all wooden bookshelves and leather chairs. It smelled strongly of cigar smoke.

Ike sat me down on a sofa then took a seat next to me. Bran plopped down in a chair on the other side.

Slowly, John Anders, Morgan Franz, Joel Westlake, Heath Barnaby, Cassian Rice, and Don Fuegos filtered in. John himself set about getting us all cognac. I noted the striking absence of a servant.

Morgan closed the door. "So, Ike, can we call this meeting to order?"

"Yes. Mr. Masterson Sr. has made his wishes known," Ike responded with a nod. "I will be representing him, as usual. Will is here to learn the ropes."

They all looked at me with varying expressions of doubt. "The football player?"

"He did also achieve a master's in business," Ike reminded them.

I wasn't sure how grateful I should be that he defended me.

"Give the man a chance. He's just getting his feet wet," Bran said, trying to smirk again.

Everyone made eye contact with his chest and not his face. "You're still in hot water, Bran. I don't know if you should be saying much of anything," Morgan chided him.

"What's he gonna do? Fry the back of my head off, too?" Bran snorted.

I realized he hadn't used the tragedy he'd suffered to grow a brain cell. I felt bad for him, for some reason. "Bran, I promise you, it is a very bad idea to tempt Grandfather into teaching you another lesson. I know from experience. You should, too."

"Well, at least that one talks sense," Heath said. "I don't suppose we can keep Will and eject Bran?"

"Hey!" Bran protested. "You will do no such thing!"

"I have no objections," Morgan said.

"I do!" Bran shot back.

Ike held up a hand. "Mr. Masterson believes Bran has been punished enough." He glared at Bran. "For now."

Bran harrumphed and crossed his arms mutinously over his chest.

"Fine then." Don took in the room then asked, "What are the new orders?"

"We're pulling out of the Iranian business. Too much unrest," Ike said.

"Thank God," Cassian replied. "That was a money pit to begin with. Whose idea was that, anyway?"

They all looked at Bran.

"What? It had great potential. Risk nothing, gain nothing." Bran defended himself.

"Uh-huh." Joel, looking much more sober, returned the conversation to Ike. "What else?"

I reluctantly raised a hand.

"Will?" Ike asked. "You have something to add?"

"I'm... sure I don't want to know this, but have to know about it anyway..." I began.

Bran chuckled. "We were trying to entice the Iranians into buying nuclear waste from us."

I blinked at him. "You were going to sell nuclear materials to Iran?!"

"For the right price. But we just couldn't get them to bite." Bran sighed.

"*You* couldn't get them to bite," Cassian corrected him.

Bran pouted. Or tried to. It didn't quite turn out to be a pout. "I gave it my best shot, okay?!"

"Gentlemen! Mr. Masterson has already dealt with Bran for a multitude of failures, not the least of which being his ill-advised assault on Will fiancée. He believes Bran might learn from this experience." Ike pursed his lips. "On some level."

I barely managed to hide a snort with a cough.

It didn't fool the other men, who smirked at me.

"Now, to the business in Guatemala. As you know, the new national policy is making it even more difficult for us to be involved in the illegal adoption business," Ike went on.

My stomach clenched. "You mean the one where kids are kidnapped out of hospitals, off the streets, and out of the arms of their parents so that they can be adopted out to American couples who have no damn clue they were stolen?"

"I love it when he sounds so sanctimonious. It's cute," Ike chuckled.

Morgan tapped my knee. "Don't think of it that way. The kidnappings and illegal adoptions were already happening. We're just benefitting from it. Someone should."

I was going to be violently sick after this meeting was over, I just knew it. But seeing Bran looking at me with that smug, well, smugish, expression on his face made me swallow the bile rising in my throat. "Do continue, Ike. I'm just *fascinated.*"

The whole room laughed, except for Bran and me.

Ike smiled and said, "We're going to have to raise our prices for our help. Also, that alcalde in the district of San Pedro los Santos is being too obvious about disappearing the women of his political rivals. I mean, they're beautiful and great additions to the sex trade, don't get me wrong, but he's starting to draw attention. He's been cautioned twice, but he hasn't corrected himself. Mr. Masterson is open to suggestions of how to deal with him."

"I'm sorry, the mayor is disappearing the female family members of his political rivals and we want to be involved in that?" I interrupted.

"Yes. We keep him on a short leash, and he provides us with slaves. There a lot of volunteers through organizations such as the Peace Corps and Doctors Without Borders who go to that area to help. We don't want him kidnapping Americans, now do we?" Ike said.

"I don't suppose we can just back one of his rivals instead?" I suggested.

The room went quiet. Ike looked impressed. "We absolutely could. It might get a little messy, and they will surely evacuate volunteers from the area until the dust settles, but... that's not a bad idea, Will."

"I thought it seemed rather obvious." Bran sniffed.

"And yet *you* didn't come up with it," Morgan said. "I like the idea. We've been dealing with that bastard far too long."

"He's a pompous little shit to talk to, too," Don grumbled.

"Who, Bran?" Cassian grinned.

Everyone chuckled except for Bran.

"No," Don said once he'd recovered himself. "The alcalde."

"Yes, let's send in a strike team. Gather up his women, as well. I think he has three little girls?" Ike mused. "And shall we kill the two sons? I so hate familial vengeance coming back to bite us in the ass."

"Wait, what?!" I gaped.

Ike patted my hand. "It's all right, Will. This is just the way things are done."

"His *kids*?! *SERIOUSLY?!!!*" I objected.

"Yes, Will. Everything has collateral damage. Even above-board business," Ike said patiently.

I couldn't take it anymore. I stood and made a beeline for the door.

"Will?" John asked.

"I'm going to be sick," I managed, yanking the door open and running out.

"Bathroom's upstairs and to the left!" John called.

I could hear Bran's cackling laugh drift up behind me.

TWENTY

PRETTY PINK ROSES

McKenzie

I saw Will trying to get to me, but being intercepted by first Bran, then Ike. Ike ultimately took him away, with several other men, including Bran, walking into the house after them.

It was a lovely summer day, and the women sitting around me were nice enough, but there was only so much interest I could show in lavish vacations, jewelry, fashion shows, etc., etc. I was bored to tears by an hour in, and I was trapped.

I also didn't have Mom. Unexpectedly, Ike had told her this morning that, instead of coming to the engagement party, she could go see Dad. Though she asked me first, in my mind, there was no question. She should go see Dad. We were all very worried about him.

Except now I was also worried about Will and all the men who'd converged on him. It ate at me, and after half an hour, I couldn't stand it anymore.

"Excuse me," I said with a polite smile. "I need to powder my nose."

The women giggled. "Sure. And check in with the housekeeper

as well, won't you?" Tracy Franz asked. "I don't think the waiters are making enough rounds with the food and champagne."

"Right," I agreed. Then I hurried away before someone could launch into the story of how their father bought a boat that was bigger than the other girl's father's boat.

I all but ran into the house, courtesy of Ike allowing me to wear flats, just in time to see Will burst out of a room and run up the stairs.

"Will?" I called after him. But he didn't hear me.

I ran upstairs after him, turning to the left when I heard a door slam. When I got to the door, there was the unmistakable sound of retching.

Panic seized my heart. "Will!" I knocked on the door. "Will, are you okay? Did they drug you?!"

"Just a second," he replied gruffly.

I waited. The toilet flushed. There was a lot of rinsing and spitting. Then the door opened. "Will—!"

He grabbed me and yanked me inside, closing the door behind me and locking it. "I need you," he said without preamble.

"What happened?" I asked, touching his cheek.

Will kissed my palm then pulled my hand down to his chest, placing it over his heart. "Tell me I'm a good man."

"You're a good man, Will," I whispered, even more worried than before. I rubbed his chest, not knowing the reason but knowing his heart must hurt.

He buried his face in my neck and sighed. "I think I just got a few villages killed."

"Villagers?" I clarified.

Will swallowed. "No."

"Oh... my love." I wrapped my arms around his neck, tangling my fingers in his hair. "It's not your fault. Those are all your grandfather's cronies, aren't they?"

He nodded.

"They made you do something you didn't want to do. They

forced you or they tricked you, but either way, it's not your fault," I said fiercely.

Will was quiet for a while, then his fingers fumbled with the zipper at the back of my dress.

He needed something else, too.

I saved him the trouble. I gave him a little push then shoved my clothes—dress, strapless bra, panties, and all—to the floor. The dress was just loose enough that I didn't really need the zipper.

His breath caught, and he reached out to touch my breast.

I tugged him closer by the waistband of his pants and undid them. His pants and boxers fell to the floor with very little encouragement.

With a frown, I asked, "Are you losing weight?"

"You are, too," he answered softly. He stroked his fingertips down my side. "My poor honeybee."

"We've both been really stressed out. And we've been through a lot," I pointed out, kissing his collarbone. I rubbed his dick, even though he was fully erect.

Will groaned. "It's still not okay. I don't want you to get sick."

"I don't want *you* to get sick!" I echoed.

"Then let's try not getting sick together." He stopped my hand. "Maybe we shouldn't. What if it's too much for you?"

"It wasn't last night," I scoffed.

"Yes, but...."

I put a finger over his lips. "I feel fine. And if you don't fuck me soon, I'm going to die."

He laughed and kissed me. "Whatever you say, honeybee." He backed me up against the door.

It was my turn to laugh. "What is it with us and bathrooms?"

"We'll make it our thing. Everywhere we go, we have to bang each other's brains out in the bathroom," he said, lifting me up and setting me down on his dick.

I moaned loudly. "That's-that's almost a poem!"

"I thought it sounded romantic," he agreed. He gripped my ass and started thrusting, fucking me hard against the door.

I clung to his shoulders, my back rubbing against the heavy wooden door with every forceful thrust. I wondered if you could get rug burn from a door. *What would you call it? Door burn?*

Then I had no thoughts at all as Will lit up my world. I cried out, not really caring who could hear me. I didn't give a damn what any of these people thought of me.

He came as well, pushing in deep. When he finished, he rested his forehead on my collarbone. "I love you so much," he whispered.

"I love you, too," I said, stroking his hair.

There was a knock on the door. "Will? McKenzie? I suggest you finish up in there. We can't continue the festivities without the guests of honor." Ike sounded amused.

I scowled at the door while Will sighed and gently pulled out, setting me down on the floor. "We'll be just a minute," he said.

"Oh! And the others loved your idea. We put it to a vote while you were gone. The transition will be happening on Monday. We've already got forces on the ground just waiting for orders," Ike continued.

Will looked sick again. "Great," he managed.

"You'll get the hang of this yet! I have every faith in you." Then I heard Ike walking away.

I cupped Will's face in my hands. "Not. Your. Fault."

"It sure feels like it is." He kissed me then just held me in his arms like an emotional support blanket.

I leaned into him and wrapped my arms around him, trying to get as close as possible.

We stayed that way for a long time.

Knocking came again, this time louder.

"Will and McKenzie! Honestly. Get out here and be sociable," Ike barked.

We looked at each other then at the door in irritation.

"We're almost there," Will said.

"How many times do you plan to do it?! After last night, I'm surprised either of you had anything left to give!" Ike complained.

"For Christsake, we're not fucking, you sick fuck. We're having a conversation!" Will snapped.

Ike actually laughed! "Temper, temper! All right, but make it quick. People are waiting downstairs." He didn't walk away this time.

Will muttered under his breath about Ike's lesser qualities while he cleaned me up and helped me back into my clothes. He then stepped into his pants and boxers, still too easily for my liking, and took my hand.

I gave myself one quick glance in the mirror, noting my hair wasn't as mussed as I thought it would be. Then we went out into the hall.

"Finally!" Ike turned on his heel and started down the stairs, expecting us to follow him.

We did.

As it turned out, we were needed for the gift opening.

Will and I sat side-by-side on a white wrought iron bench outside and spent the next two hours opening gifts and thanking people. I could hardly believe the things we got. Vacations, both at other people's vacation properties and not. Jewelry I'd be too frightened to wear in case someone might steal it. Three expensive cars. And a yacht.

"It's just a small yacht," Joel Westlake said apologetically. "Just sixty meters."

"Joel, there are only eighteen yachts in the world that are between sixty and seventy meters. It's a perfectly lovely gift," Ike replied. "Besides, the Mastersons already have a super yacht. This one will be a nice recreation craft."

"It's a lovely gift," I assured Joel, feeling a little bad for the alcoholic. He clearly was one.

He perked up a bit. "I suppose you're right. Please, enjoy the gift. Sail around the whole world."

That wasn't going to be happening. With the way Ike kept an eye on us?

"I can't wait!" I replied, forcing some enthusiasm into my tone.

"Let's move on, shall we?" Ike said, handing me another gift. The paper was baby blue with a thick, white ribbon. "This one is from Mr. Masterson. He regrets being unable to be here in person."

No one dared to laugh.

I smiled. "I'll have to thank him the next time we visit." I opened the box and pulled out a baby boy's sailor suit, complete with a little hat and shoes. "O-kay...."

Will plucked the clothes from my fingers, looking them over. "Wishful thinking?"

"Just a little inspiration." Ike grinned. "You're getting married soon, after all."

"I think we discussed holding off on children for a short while. But thank Grandfather for the thoughtful gift, if we don't see him first. We'll be sure to keep it for *if* and when we have a boy," Will said, his tone icy.

I elbowed him in the side. "Of course, it's adorable. He has very good taste in baby clothes."

"Doesn't he just? We'll discuss the details later. I'm sure you're both very excited to become parents," Ike stated.

Something was wrong. Will knew something was wrong, too. I gripped his hand when he started to stand. "Will," I whispered. "The gifts. We'll talk to him later."

It took a moment, but he finally backed down. The tension didn't leave his body, however.

Once the gift opening had finished, the crowd moved on to see a famous comedian who had been hired privately for the event.

Will dragged me off the bench, and we quickly cornered Ike near some rose bushes before he could escape.

"What is the meaning of the baby clothes?" Will demanded.

Ike chuckled. "You really can't figure it out, can you?"

"A clue would be nice," Will seethed.

"You don't need a clue," Ike said.

I swallowed. "Am I... not going to college?"

"Oh, you certainly are, my dear," Ike replied before Will could get a word in. "Just after the baby is born."

"Fuck that! Ike, Grandfather cannot be serious. One, McKenzie is nineteen. *Nineteen*. She has no business having a baby right now! Two, you can't guarantee the child will be a boy! It's insane to think that's possible. Three—" Will ticked off his points until Ike interrupted.

"There are ways to guarantee a boy. In vitro fertilization, for instance," Ike said.

"No." Will shook his head. "Absolutely not."

Ike shrugged. "Then I guess you keep having babies until McKenzie has a boy. It's a rather simple concept, Will."

"I won't let that happen. No children until she's done with school," Will said firmly.

"Um... I'm right here," I mumbled. "But I agree. It's too soon."

"It was too soon. Then you started galavanting around the countryside with your friends. Now, Mr. Masterson wants guarantees. You can raise your child, or he can, but it's happening," Ike stated.

Will frowned. "Once we have that boy, Grandfather is going to take him away anyway. He won't want either of us raising him."

Horror overwhelmed my system. "What?"

Ike smiled. "You're a very smart boy, Will."

"I won't let that happen," Will said again.

"Well, technically you don't have to. We still have your father's sperm from the last time and Jacey is still... serviceable."

"She's forty-eight!" I cried. "Wait, why did you suddenly decide this morning that Mom didn't need to be here and should go visit Dad?"

Ike smiled again.

"Will?" I whispered, grabbing his arm.

"Ike. Tell me you didn't," Will breathed.

Ike shrugged. "She did such a beautiful job last time."

Something snapped in Will. I could feel it in the air. He surged forward and grabbed Ike by the throat.

Ike gurgled, clawing at Will's hand and wrist.

"Will!" I put myself between them and tugged on his arm. "Will, no!"

"He can't keep doing these things without consequences," Will hissed. "He's fucking having your mother violated, for Christsake!"

Tears stung my eyes at his statement, but I held firm. "Will, this isn't the way. They'll hurt the others. You know they will. Every time we do something, he does something even more horrible. You can't do this."

Will's chest rose and fell rapidly. He was beyond angry. He was beyond rage. I thought he'd reached a level of upset that didn't have a name!

Then, much to my relief, and small disappointment, he let Ike go.

Ike stumbled back into a rose bush clutching his throat.

"McKenzie's going to college," Will said, his voice dripping darkness. "And you're going to stop whatever you're doing with Jacey. Or so help me, Ike, I will make *sure* Grandfather's empire falls down around his ears."

Ike just nodded, incapable of speech.

Will put his arm around me, and we walked away.

Behind me, I thought I heard Ike on his phone:

"Yes, sir. I think if we keep pushing, everything will fall right into place."

TWENTY-ONE

THE BREAKING POINT

Will

I pretended to laugh at the famous comedian, even though I didn't give a flying fuck about his jokes and was barely listening to him anyway. McKenzie was beside me, fake smiling and clapping, even though there was a mist of tears in her eyes.

That was going to break me. It wasn't going to be the fuckery with her family or our friends. It wasn't going to be forcing me into making decisions that would destroy countless lives. It was going to be seeing McKenzie slowly worn away into obedience.

Why the fuck *did I ever think 'being good' was the solution?!* Being good was going to shatter all of us, but especially McKenzie. And I couldn't abide that.

My scrappy, sassy source of love and comfort was *not* going to become a baby factory for that money-grubbing, power hungry asshole I called my grandfather. And neither was Jacey.

I couldn't even imagine what kind of lives those children would have or what would become of us once Grandfather had children to leverage us with.

No, no, no, no, *no*.

McKenzie tapped my thigh, and I realized the comedian had finished and everyone was clapping. I smiled and clapped as well.

"I suppose the next step is to cut the cake?" she asked softly, still pale.

"No," I said, finally fucking fed up. "The next step is us leaving."

"Leaving?" She sounded confused. "What do you mean? There's a huge cake. I figured they'd expect us to cut it."

"I am done with what people expect. Neither of us is in a fit state to stick around. We're leaving." I tugged on her hand, heading out of the yard and up toward the mansion.

She panicked. "Will, we can't! Mom and Dad! Dolly and Shep! Moose!"

"They're in danger no matter what we do. McKenzie, nothing is going to change unless *we* change it." I took a deep breath. "We're going to the Feds."

"The FBI?!" She gaped at me. "They've almost gotten my parents killed like a hundred times!"

"I guess we're going to be time a-hundred-and-one. We're not playing this game anymore. It's never going to end if we don't end it," I said.

McKenzie pulled me to a stop. "No. This is insanity. They'll kill someone. Probably Dad. I won't do this."

With a sigh, I dragged her the rest of the way into the mansion. I pressed her back against a wall with my body and tipped her chin up, forcing her to look at me. "Honeybee, what kind of life are we consigning them to if we do nothing? Hm? Jacey perpetually pregnant with my dad's genetic material? Your dad, Moose, and Shep lying on a concrete slab for the rest of their days, waiting to be taken out and dangled over us at a moment's notice? Dolly locked in her room, unable to see any of them? Hell, *us* being unable to see any of them? Not to mention what's going to be done to you. And you want me to stand still, wringing my hands, saying, 'Oh well, it could be worse' until it does get worse? It's going to keep getting worse and worse, McKenzie, until there's nothing left of any of us."

Her tears flowed over. "I don't want anyone to die."

"I know, honeybee. I don't, either. But this might be our one shot." I thumbed her tears away and waited for her decision. If she decided to bow under Grandfather's pressure... I knew it would kill me, but I would still have to go. I had to try to stop this before it was too late.

"You'll go without me, won't you?" she whispered, staring into my eyes.

I swallowed and nodded. "I can't let them keep hurting people. Especially you."

"What if you going to the FBI gets me killed?" she asked.

My eyes stung, my heart seizing at the very thought. "McKenzie, please...."

She kissed me. "I love you, Will."

My heart sank. "Oh God...."

"And I'll go with you."

Relief washed over me like warm rain, and I wrapped her in my arms. "Okay. Okay, good. But we have to go now."

McKenzie nodded and took my hand.

We walked to the front door and then out into the circle drive. A valet saw us and jumped. "Miss Kent? Mr. Masterson?"

"Yes. We'd like the keys to the convertible we were just gifted. We thought we'd take it for a spin," I said, holding out my hand.

"What, now?" the valet asked, perplexed.

"Yes. We need a little alone time." I winked at him.

He scratched the back of his neck. "I'm not really supposed to give you the keys."

"To the convertible?" I asked.

"To... well... anything. I have orders," he said.

I sighed. "What would it take to ignore those orders?" I went for my watch.

McKenzie unclipped her earrings.

The valet licked his lips. "Yeah, those'll do."

"Good." I dropped my watch into his hand then waited expectantly. "No keys, no earrings."

"Right." The valet unlocked a box behind him and took out a key. "This is to that Jaguar over there. I know it's not yours, but it's parked in a spot you can actually get out of without running over six other cars."

I snatched the key. "Thank you."

McKenzie dropped her earrings into his hand.

Then I took her hand again, and we made a run for it.

Things went smoothly as I pulled out and headed for the gate. Then I saw Ike in the rearview mirror coming out the front door.

He slapped the valet across the face then grabbed a remote and pointed it at the gate.

The gate started to close.

I looked at McKenzie. McKenzie looked at me.

Then I floored it.

We shot past the bars, flying through.

The gate brushed the back of the car, taking off a good layer or two of paint, I was sure, but we made it.

I narrowly missed a lamppost as we hit a sharp curve, and the Jaguar fishtailed. I managed to get the car back under control.

Then I rolled down my window. "Dump your phone."

I dropped my phone out of the window, and McKenzie did so as well.

"They're going to guess where we're going, aren't they?" she asked.

"Probably. But we're going to try to get there anyway," I said.

"You know where we're going?" She sounded surprised.

I nodded. "I tried once before, but I think my grandfather had people posing as agents stationed there to intercept me. I don't think he'll have time to make arrangements now, and even if he does, this time, I'll raise a ruckus."

"That works." She threaded her fingers through mine. I rested our joined hands on her thigh.

We drove in silence from then on. No police chased us on the highway. No unmarked vans were waiting for us at the federal building in Brooklyn Center.

I half expected to see a red dot on my chest or McKenzie's when we got out of the car. But nothing that dramatic happened.

"No matter how this goes, honeybee," I said quietly as I took her hand again and walked us into the building, "know that I love you."

"I love you, too. Always and forever," she replied with a swallow.

A security guard stopped us. "Can I help you?"

I squared my shoulders. "My name is William Masterson the Third, and this is McKenzie Killeen. We'd like to speak to someone about an illegal high society crime ring."

The guard blinked then snorted. "You want to what now?" he chuckled.

"Just... wait for it," I said, glancing up at a camera.

He shook his head. "Go on, you two. Go tell your story to someone who's going to believe that bullsh—"

A man in a suit, flanked by two other guards, appeared and came stalking up to us. "That will do, Thurmes. Back to your station."

"Sir, it's just another conspiracy wingnut like they told us to be looking out for," Thurmes replied.

"*Who* told you, Thurmes?" the man asked coldly.

Thurmes seemed to realize then that he might be in deep shit. "The police officers from before."

"From before?" the man pressed.

"Yeah. They came and said—"

The man sighed, pinching the bridge of his nose. "I'm not going to begin to explain to you what an idiot you are. You have a supervisor for that. Mr. Masterson, Miss Killeen, please come with me."

The other guards flanked us so there wasn't really a choice in the matter.

"We're all in now," I murmured to McKenzie.

"We are," she agreed.

As we walked down a hall, then took an elevator upstairs, the man in the suit didn't say a word. It wasn't until we were in an office I presumed to be his that he finally spoke.

"My name is Daniel Wilson. I'll be taking charge of your case until the new attorney general arrives from Washington," he droned. "I've been instructed to collect your statements. I realize that could take a very long time."

"William Masterson Sr. has taken our family and friends hostage," I said before he could continue. "They need help."

"We don't even know for sure where they are," McKenzie added.

Wilson paused. "It will be hard for us to mount a raid if we don't know where to look."

"Can you... I don't know... waterboard my grandfather or Ike Freeborn or something?" I asked desperately.

"Trust me. I would love to. We'll question them, of course, but that hasn't worked in the past." He sighed.

"We're worried about what will happen to them because we've come in," McKenzie pleaded. "Please. Isn't there anything you can do?"

"I can send teams to search all known properties of Mr. Masterson Sr. but his lawyer will fight any warrants, which will give them plenty of time to move them to a property we know nothing about. If they haven't done that already. The legal elements of all of this move quite slowly, I'm afraid. I wouldn't be surprised if your grandfather's lawyers are already poised to fight the warrants." Wilson looked as frustrated as I felt. "I'll get a colleague to see what we can do, but realistically, it's very unlikely we'll be able to recover those people for a long, long time."

Still, this didn't sound right to me. "How long is a long, long time?"

"Years," he said. "Likely several years."

During which time my grandfather would probably force Jacey to give birth at least once. Or kill her. Or both.

"Maybe this was a mistake," McKenzie whispered, tugging on

my arm. "I think we should go back before Ike and your grandfather get really, really mad."

He raised an eyebrow at us. "You really think you can un-pull that trigger?"

She bit her lip. "I didn't think there would be nothing you could do for our family and friends."

"I don't think we *can* go back at this point, McKenzie," I said, feeling awful. It was a damned if we do, damned if we don't situation. I knew it would be, but I'd at least expected the FBI could do... something.

She raised her chin. "Then I've made a decision."

This can't be good. I looked at Wilson and knew we shared the same thought.

"I won't testify until our family and friends are safe." She added a firm nod to show how serious she was.

He grimaced. "That's a tall order, Miss Killeen."

Actually, it wasn't a bad idea. I put my arm around her shoulders. "I won't either. We're taking a big risk. Considering how well you did with Caleb and Jacey, a *very* big risk. So, in return, you need to step up."

"We don't even know where they are," he argued.

"Tough. Get some men on it. Until then, our lips are sealed," I said.

McKenzie gave me a grateful smile, sliding her arm around my waist.

"Ugh. This case, I swear." He reached in his pocket and pulled out his phone. "I'll make some calls. I can't make any promises, but I'll try. You're going to be taken to separate interview rooms. I'll be there when I can."

"Separate?" I protested. "No. McKenzie and I don't do separate."

"Tough." Wilson repeated my earlier word.

Then she and I were physically wrenched apart by the guards.

TWENTY-TWO
SEPARATED

McKenzie

The room was cold.

Furniture from some random office supply store or another was arranged to make it feel more 'homey,' I'm sure. But it was cold, completely devoid of personality.

Plus some dickhead had set the thermostat too low. *Maybe it's supposed to help make people talk?*

The security guard who'd grabbed me away from Will was standing just outside the door. I could see him through the small window.

That's how I knew Agent Wilson was coming. At least, I thought he was an agent. He hadn't really introduced himself as anything except the attorney general's minion.

He let himself in, closing the door behind him. The security guard locked us inside.

"Miss Killeen," Wilson said, sitting down across from me at the table, "would you be more comfortable on one of the couches? This doesn't have to be an interrogation."

"It will be until Will and I are together again," I replied waspishly. But I didn't care if I sounded like a raging bitch.

He sighed. "Very well." He set a phone down between us. "I'll be recording our conversation. Is that all right?"

"Whatever gets me back to Will faster." My tone sounded like I didn't care about his stupid interrogation.

I didn't.

"Can you please state your name for the record?" he asked.

"McKenzie Ann Kent," I responded. "Though most people say my last name is really Killeen."

"Can you explain that further?" he pressed.

I pursed my lips. This was clearly going to be long and tedious. "My parents are Jocelyn Collins and Caleb Killeen. But when they got married, they took the name Kent because they were in hiding from William Masterson Sr. So, technically, my last name is Kent, but it would have been Killeen if my parents weren't on the run."

"Your parents changed their identities and yours for your family's safety?" He looked at me expectantly.

"Yes..." I said, not knowing what he wanted to hear.

"Do you know why Mr. Masterson Sr. was persecuting your family?" he asked.

I frowned. "Everyone knows why. I'm sure my parents told you themselves when they were in your custody."

"Please tell me anyway. In your own words," he said.

I fought the urge to roll my eyes. "I was told this secondhand by Will, so it might be better to get it from him. But my parents stumbled upon an illegal logging operation while camping in Canada. It all went downhill from there. Ultimately, they discovered a whole host of illegal businesses that Masterson had his hands in. Human trafficking. Drugs. Weapons. You name it! Masterson tried to keep my parents under lock and key, but they came to you guys at great personal risk. Guess how well *that* turned out?"

"For the record, Mr. and Mrs. Kent were removed from FBI

custody illegally while recuperating at a hospital for wounds sustained from a bombing in Oakdale, Minnesota," he inserted.

"It was definitely Masterson," I insisted. "Ike was so smug about it. I mean, he never admitted it outright, but he heavily implied it was Masterson."

"Ike Freeborn?" he clarified.

"Yes." God, this was going to be even more painful than I originally thought!

Wilson leaned over the phone again. "For the record, Ike Freeborn is a known associate of William Masterson Sr. and is believed to be carrying out his wishes and running his businesses in Mr. Masterson's absence."

"Oh, that I *know* he's doing," I confirmed. "Most definitely."

"How do you know?" he asked.

"He told me. And Will's told me." I try not to scream in frustration. "Speaking of Will, are we done yet?"

Wilson laughed. "Not even half. But nice try."

"I want to see Will," I argued.

"You'll see him after I've interviewed you both." He went back to his questions. "When did you first learn about Mr. Masterson?"

"Seriously?! We're going back *that* far?!" I groaned and banged my head on the tabletop. "This is going to take forever!"

"It will take as long as it takes. Please answer the question." He was unmoved.

I opened my mouth, not sure if I was going to answer his question or say something smart.

But just then, there was a loud **BANG**.

I jumped.

Wilson shot out of his chair and went to the door. "McNamara, what's going on?!"

The security guard didn't answer. He couldn't.

I gasped as McNamara slid down the door, leaving a streak of blood on the window.

"Shit!" Wilson came back and flipped the table on its side. He pulled me behind it, using it as a barrier between us and the door.

Another **BANG** made my heart slam against my ribcage. I was terrified for Will. I wanted him beside me right now, not this suit.

Wilson pulled a gun out of a holster under his jacket and pointed it at the door. "No matter what happens, stay down."

"Yes, sir," I replied. And I was happy to do so until a third **BANG** ripped through the air. Smoke came pouring into the room and around the table.

He coughed and pulled his shirt up over his nose and mouth.

I couldn't do the same with the scoop-necked dress I was wearing and just started coughing, beginning to stand to get above the worst of it.

"Stay down!" he repeated. He quickly shrugged out of his jacket and tossed it over my head.

I tried to breathe through the heavy fabric, but it was suffocating. Still, I didn't want to get shot, so I did my best.

Finally, I heard the door open.

There was another loud **BANG** as Wilson shot whoever came in. At least, that was what I thought had happened until he dropped to the floor next to me. I pushed the jacket up just far enough to see his glassy eyes, a bleeding hole in his head.

I scrabbled for his gun, but a booted foot kicked it away.

Without saying a word, the person, wearing all black with a gas mask over their face, handed me a mask of my own.

I gulped and put it on.

The person gently adjusted it, and soon, I was breathing more easily. Then they grabbed my arm and hauled me up off the floor.

There were more black-clad mercenaries out in the hall and several dead agents. I saw Will dragged out of another interview room, stepping over the body of the other security guard I recognized.

The strange assassins marched Will and me to the stairwell then back down to the first floor. To my absolute shock, we walked right out the front door. I hoped the people I saw hunched over here and there were just drugged and not dead.

Will was put in a black SUV. I began to follow him, but the person who gave me the gas mask pulled me back and shook their head.

It was then I realized Will and I were being separated for real.

I tried to tear through the mercenaries to get to him, just as Will tried to push his way out of the SUV to get to me. We were both thwarted by the black-clad bastards who forced me into a silver sedan.

"Mr. Masterson," I heard one say before they closed my door, "get back in the SUV."

I looked out the window and gasped. They were holding guns on him!

Wait, when did Will get that gun?!

I wasn't sure how Will responded. His lips moved, but I couldn't hear him.

I jiggled the handle on my door but wasn't surprised to find that the child lock was on. I couldn't get out on my own.

Then, to my surprise, the mercenary next to my door opened it. They reached in and yanked me out.

And put a gun to my head.

"Are you done yet?" the lead mercenary asked Will.

Will's hand shook.

The gun dug harder into my temple, and I yelped.

"McKenzie!" he cried. He looked around at all the black-clad assholes who surrounded us. Then he put the gun to his own head.

"*NO!!!*" I screamed.

"William." The voice was patient but firm. "Please don't disappoint me like your father did."

I couldn't help myself. Despite the gun at my temple, I whipped my head around.

There stood William Masterson Sr., wearing a suit, radiating infinite calm. He wasn't a bit fazed.

I, on the other hand, was freaking out. "Masterson?!"

"Mr. Masterson, dear. But you'll get used to it." Masterson walked through the mercenaries as though they were nothing but brushes in a car wash and stood right before Will. "Give me the gun, Will."

Will turned the gun on Masterson, his face a mask of hatred.

Masterson sighed. "Oh, Will. You just don't think ahead. What do you think will happen to McKenzie if you shoot me?"

"A lot less than will happen if I don't," Will said coldly.

"I know. I know we've been a bit hard on you, Will. But I'm not a monster. I'm not going to hurt McKenzie. I'll even let her go to school before having children. It was wrong of me to take that away from her." Masterson smiled reassuringly. "I've scared you, I know. That's why you keep acting out."

"You *are* a monster, and I don't believe one goddamn *fucking* word that comes out of your mouth!" Will shouted, his gun not wavering.

Masterson raised an eyebrow. "Will. Such vitriol. All right. How about this? If you kill me, or yourself, I will have McKenzie violated in ways you cannot possibly imagine. Then I will have Jacey pump out enough brothers and sisters this time that I'm sure *one* of them will be properly groomed to the position I want you to take. I'd make that my plan, but I don't trust Ike to carry out my wishes once I'm gone. That's the *only* reason I've put up with your shenanigans."

I felt sick. Part of me wanted Will to shoot Masterson and damn the consequences. Another part was worried about my mother becoming a baby factory at the age of forty-eight. Most of me was worried about Will. However this standoff ended, what would happen to him? To us?

"McKenzie," Masterson said, still completely unbothered, "now might be a good time to make your wishes known."

Will looked at me.

It was a mistake. "No, Will, don't!"

Masterson snatched the gun out of Will's hand and handed it to one of the mercenaries at his side. "Oh, Will." He gripped his grandson by the hair and slammed his face into the side of the SUV. "You really are quite stupid sometimes."

"Leave him alone!" I snarled, still caring very little about the gun pointed at my head. When I saw Will being manhandled like that, I didn't even remember it was there.

"McKenzie." Masterson gave me the long once-over as Will was shoved in the SUV. "I'm not sure if you're the biggest pain in the ass I've ever had or the greatest asset I've ever had."

I broke free of the mercenary holding me. They could shoot me for all I cared. I had to get to Will.

"Ames," Masterson said blandly, "shoot her."

TWENTY-THREE
BANG-BANG

Will

Shoot her. My heart stopped.

I kicked the man shoving me into the SUV in the knee. It gave a satisfying pop, and he went down.

Crawling over him, I scrambled out of the SUV. But I was too late.

A shot rang out.

"No!" I screamed.

But McKenzie didn't fall to the ground.

Ames did.

I stopped next to my grandfather, who was staring in just as much confusion as I was. "Carlson, what the hell—?" Grandfather snapped.

Carlson, or who I assumed was Carlson, turned to face my grandfather.

Then Carlson was gone, too, in a spray of blood.

The mercenaries surrounded us, herding McKenzie, Grandfather, and me to the middle of a phalanx. I hugged McKenzie to me and ducked down. I didn't give a fuck what my grandfather decided to do.

"Is it the police?" one of the mercenaries asked my grandfather.

"No. I paid them handsomely to stay away and to keep others away as well," Grandfather said.

That mercenary nodded. It was the last thing he ever did.

Once he was on the ground, the other mercenaries began to panic. "Fuck this shit!" one snarled. "I'm getting the *fuck* out of here!" He headed to the SUV.

Two others followed him.

Whoever was shooting fired at the SUV and at them. All three went down, and the SUV's engine wheezed, then died, having been shot twice. In an act of overkill, the shooter took out the SUV's tires as well.

"Christ." My grandfather grabbed one of the mercenaries and used him as a human shield to get to the sedan.

It worked—to a degree. The unwilling mercenary became riddled with bullets while my grandfather skidded into the driver's seat of the sedan. It was all for naught, however, because suddenly that engine was obliterated as well as the car tires.

"*Fuck!*" my grandfather exclaimed, getting out of the sedan and crouching next to it.

The rest of the mercenaries decided they were done being fish in a barrel. They took off down the street to a line of vehicles parked further away, leaving McKenzie and me completely exposed. I held her tightly, praying we weren't next.

"I'm havin' trouble decidin' whether or not to shoot the bastard," a familiar voice said behind us.

I turned my head. "Moose?!"

Moose stood with a rifle slung over his back and a Glock in his hand, pointing it directly at Grandfather. "Seems a waste to just let him walk away."

"Moose!" McKenzie shot up out of my arms and hugged the grizzled veteran. "Thank God! Where's Mom and Dad? And Dolly and Shep? Are Dad and Shep okay?"

"It was a hell of a thing gettin' them out of that place, but they're restin'. I think they'll be okay," he said. "The reason that one ain't dead is we don't know where Dolly is."

"She was at the estate," I informed him. "Have you managed to get in there?"

He snorted. "Your parents make it sound like a death trap. Yeah, that don't sound like somewhere you just walk into."

I looked at my grandfather. "I can think of someone who can get us in and out without any trouble."

"Why would I help you?" Grandfather scoffed.

Moose gently pushed McKenzie aside and pointed his gun at him. "I have a Glock. My Glock says you want to be helpful."

"He has a gun, too," I murmured. "I'd bet my life on it. He gave the one he took off of me to one of the others, but I am sure he still has one of his own.."

"Well, ain't that special." Moose kept the Glock pointed unflinchingly at my grandfather. "Gun, please."

With a low growl, Grandfather tossed it over.

"Great. Now we're all goin' to get in my goddamn truck. Will, you take that gun and cover him from the back. I'm drivin'." Moose pointed to a rusty red pick-up parked around the side of the building.

The convoy of mercenaries took off, taking with them Grandfather's last shred of hope. I found it very satisfying.

My grandfather got out from behind the sedan and followed Moose to the truck with McKenzie and me walking behind him. I had the gun trained on the back of his head.

Moose opened the passenger door and pulled the seat forward so McKenzie, and I could get in. Once we were situated, he pushed the seat back and waved my grandfather inside. "Keep that gun trained right on him. No distractions this time," Moose said sternly.

I winced. *So, he saw that.* "Yes, sir."

He slammed Grandfather's door shut and stomped to the other side of the truck.

"You're going to regret this, Will," my grandfather seethed.

"I doubt it," I replied, not letting the gun waver an inch.

Moose hopped into the driver's seat then got settled, transferring the gun to his left hand and holding it in his lap, pointed right at my grandfather's guts. "Don't be thinkin' I ain't just as skilled with my left hand. You fuck around, you're gonna find out."

"I understand," Grandfather said.

"Will, you put that pistol down where the cops can't see it. It should still shoot through the seat just fine if need be," Moose instructed me.

I lowered the gun and pointed it at the back of my grandfather's seat.

"You do know you're all just going to suffer more for this poor decision?" Grandfather warned.

Moose pulled away from the curb. "They always say the same bullshit. Like their brains ain't gonna be the same color splatted on the ground as anybody else's."

I poked my grandfather in the shoulder. "Call Ike. Tell him to bring Dolly wherever Moose asks to meet."

"I most certainly will not!" Grandfather snorted.

Moose loudly cocked his gun. "I'm thinkin' Will has the right idea."

My grandfather huffed. "He'll never agree to it. I've taught him better than that."

"We'll see." I poked him again. "I think it's worth a try."

Grandfather rolled his eyes and pulled out his phone.

"Put it on speaker," Moose said.

My grandfather put the phone on speaker. It rang just once before Ike picked up. "Sir?"

"I've been kidnapped. Why didn't you tell me they'd escaped the facility?!" Grandfather roared.

"I don't have any intel to that effect, sir. What do you mean they've escaped? We're getting check-ins at regular intervals...." Ike trailed off. "They're with you, sir?"

"That asshole they call Moose just ruined the *entire* operation! And now they're holding me hostage until I can produce Dolly." My grandfather was incensed.

Ike took a deep breath. "Sir, I've been told on many occasions not to succumb to blackmail."

"That's what I told them!" Grandfather was breathing hard now. "I know you'll put Dolly down a deep, dark hole until the end of time for whatever they're about to do to me. No mercy."

"Of course, sir." Ike hung up.

"What the *fuck*?! That was it?!" I yelled.

"Will, it's unbecoming to raise your voice. Real power doesn't have to," Grandfather said.

Moose was quiet. Dangerously quiet. He lowered my grandfather's window with the push of a button. "Throw the phone out."

Grandfather snorted but did as he was told, tossing the phone out.

Without a word, Moose rolled the window back up.

"Moose, what do we do?" McKenzie asked, her voice strained. "We can't let them hurt her!"

"We won't." Moose pulled onto the highway.

"I'd love to know how you're going to prevent it," my grandfather scoffed.

"You'll see." The way Moose said it sent chills down my spine.

My grandfather laughed. "You think you scare me, but you don't. You need me to have any hope of getting Dolly back. But the part you don't understand is that you're *never* going to see her again, regardless of what you do. Quite a conundrum you have there, *Moose*."

"No conundrum, Mr. Masterson. I see the situation real clear." We pulled off the highway onto a bumpy dirt road.

"Figures you would try hiding them in the middle of nowhere again," Grandfather sniffed.

"I didn't. This here's your stop. Your last stop." Moose turned sharply into a copse of trees.

"What is that supposed to m—?"

Moose whipped his Glock up from his lap and shot my grandfather in the head.

McKenzie let out a shout of surprise.

I didn't make a sound, just stared.

"Damn. Gonna have to clean that window before we head back out," Moose said calmly. He reached over my grandfather's body and swung the passenger door open, then shoved Grandfather out, letting him fall to the ground with a final thud.

"H-he's dead..." McKenzie breathed. "Oh my God, he's actually dead...."

"Sometimes that's all you can do with evil," Moose said. He took out a handkerchief and began wiping my grandfather's blood, brains, and bone off the passenger window. "Shoulda kept some wet wipes in here. Will, can I have your shirt? Not sure what I'm wearing's gonna be nearly as absorbent."

He talked as though he were doing a little light housekeeping. I unbuttoned my shirt and handed it over, staring out the window at the corpse and trying to process the situation.

"He's really dead..." she repeated.

Moose used a little spit, and my shirt and finally got the window looking presentable. "Always makes such a mess. Anyway, we'd best get outta here. There's gonna be people comin' for him. I'm sure he's got a tracker on him or in him somewhere."

"Okay." I tried to man up and sound just as nonchalant as Moose, but my voice cracked.

He looked in the back seat. "You two are gonna be fine. And I'm gettin' Dolly. All I have to find out is how many of 'em it takes."

"How many of who?" I asked.

"Your granddad's associates. Think I'll start with that Ike character," he mused.

"Right." It wasn't a bad idea. "What do you need me to do?"

Moose smiled. "I think havin' you draw them out has been goin' just fine. But I think you two are tired of it. So, if you know who all I should be targeting, that'll help. I won't need nothin' more than that."

"I can help you with that," I said. "But you're right, Ike Freeborn is your best bet."

He put the truck in gear and reversed right over my grandfather's arm. He didn't even flinch. "Then I'll start with him."

TWENTY-FOUR
THE AFFAIRS OF DRAGONS

McKenzie

I couldn't figure out how Will and Moose chatted so casually as we got back on the highway. It was as though neither of them had seen the devil killed before their very eyes.

Well, to be fair, Moose had done the actual killing, but for Will to be so unaffected boggled my mind. As much of an asshole as Masterson had been, he was still Will's grandfather. I was sure Will had to be having feelings about his grandfather's death. But instead of talking about it, he was discussing fishing spots with Moose.

"... fly-in camp in Canada," Moose was reminiscing. "Best fishin' I ever had."

"I did some salmon fishing in Alaska. That was fun," Will said.

"Never been to Alaska," Moose replied.

"Really? When all this is over, I'll take you there," Will promised.

I just stared at the two of them.

"McKenzie? You ever been fishin'?" Moose asked, looking back at me in the rearview mirror.

"You... realize a man is dead, right?" I responded slowly.

Moose and Will looked at each other. "Sure do," Moose said. "But not talkin' about fishin' ain't gonna bring him back."

"No, but... Will? He was your grandfather..." I tried.

"I'll process that later. Right now, I just want to forget about it," Will explained.

I gave up. "I fished in the Boundary Waters. It was great."

"That's the spirit." Moose grinned at me. "Can't be spendin' too much time cryin' over the devil."

I wished I could say he had some redeeming qualities. Masterson was a human being, after all. But, try as I might, I couldn't think of one thing. "I guess... you have a point."

"You can process it with Will later," Moose assured me. "I'm sure he's got some complicated feelings."

"Okay." I leaned on Will's shoulder and wrapped my arm through his. Maybe we wouldn't talk just then, but I could at least be physically there for him.

Will kissed the top of my head. "Should I even ask where we're going?"

"Always best you don't know," Moose replied.

We fell into companionable silence. I would have mortgaged a kidney to know what Will was thinking about, but I figured it was better if I didn't interrupt his thoughts.

The highway turned from four-lane to two-lane, and then there were no painted lines on the road at all. The woods thickened on either side until branches hung over the road and scraped the top and sides of the truck.

"How many hideaways do you have?" Will asked as we went down a bumpy road between the trees that was covered in tall grass.

"Man's gotta be ready for anythin'. Your life's gonna be like this, too. If you still got any money squirreled away, I'll help you hide it," Moose said.

Will's eyes widened. "Moose, if I can still get access to that money, you can have it. You've done so much for us."

Moose smiled slightly. "I'm set, Will. You're the one who's gonna need somethin' goin' forward. I can take care of Dolly, Shep, and me. You got McKenzie, Jacey, Caleb, and any little ones who might be coming."

Will's shoulders drooped. "I suppose we can't stay together, then."

"I'd like that—I really would—but you're a hot item and, no disrespect, but I'm choosin' Dolly and Shep. I'm gonna get you all set up, but then I gotta cut you loose," Moose said regretfully.

"I understand." Will hugged me tighter. "We've been nothing but trouble for all of you."

"Yeah, but you're good people. It's worth takin' care of good people as much as you can," Moose replied.

"Thank you," I said, "For everything you've done."

Moose chuckled. "We ain't partin' ways yet. You can't get rid of me that easily."

Will and I laughed a little. But I still felt sad, and I knew Will did, too. Especially since our problematic existence had led to Dolly being put down some dark hole by Ike.

The cabin we arrived at was much smaller and more rustic than Moose's other cabin. It was still situated on a lake, however, albeit a tiny one.

Mom was outside, washing something in a trough. When she saw the truck pull up with us inside, she dropped whatever it was and squealed. "Caleb! Caleb, they're here!"

Dad's head popped up through a window. I could see he was reclining in a bed. I jumped out of the truck as soon as it stopped and ran to Mom, throwing my arms around her. "Are you okay?!" I asked. "Is Dad okay? How's Shep?"

"Shep and your dad are recovering nicely. Moose really is the best nurse ever," Mom said, smiling at Moose.

Moose muttered something under his breath, but his ears turned pink with embarrassment as he stepped into the cabin.

Will came up and wrapped his arms around me from behind. "Did they... do anything to you?"

Mom's smile faltered. "They tried, but the first round was completely unsuccessful. They didn't even have to wait to see if it took. They didn't have time for another before... I don't know. Someone made a mistake and Moose... just... killed everyone."

"Everyone?" Will repeated.

"Right down to the horrid doctor," Mom confirmed. "But don't worry your sweet heads about it. It's all in the past now. Moose will get Dolly, and then we'll be just fine."

I winced.

"What?" Mom asked.

"When Moose gets Dolly, we're going our separate ways. They can't keep helping us, Mom," I said gently.

Her shoulders hunched. "Oh."

"But Moose is getting us set up first," Will added quickly. "We'll be in a good position. It'll be okay."

"I wish we'd stop losing people," Mom whispered.

My stomach twisted. "Yeah, me, too."

Will, clearly trying to lighten the situation, said, "My grandfather is dead."

Mom's head snapped up. "Masterson? Masterson is *dead*?!"

"The very one," he confirmed. His arms tightened around me.

A certain *Wizard of Oz* song played in my head, but I certainly wasn't going to mess with his feelings by singing it out loud.

She just stood there, staring at him. "Masterson is dead."

"As a doornail," Will said.

Mom stumbled back and caught herself on the trough. "He-he's dead."

"Jacey? What's the matter?" Dad called out the window.

She looked up, tears running down her face. "Masterson is dead."

Dad's eyes widened. "You're shitting me. When? How?"

"Moose shot him a couple of hours ago in that truck then pushed the body out in the middle of nowhere," I provided so Will didn't have to. "Masterson came with a bunch of mercenaries to kidnap us from federal custody, but Moose shot some of them and scared the rest off. Masterson wouldn't help us get Dolly, so... basically I guess he wasn't any use to us alive. Moose said sometimes you just have to kill evil."

"Jesus." Dad looked completely shell shocked. "I thought that man was immortal."

"I think Grandfather did, too, because he was being all cocky about it," Will said. His voice was a little scratchy, and my heart hurt for him. "Can't believe a man that smart could be such an idiot."

Mom seemed to snap out of it, then. She reached around me to squeeze Will's arm. "I know we didn't like him much, sweetheart, but I'm still very sorry for your loss."

"I mean, he brought it on himself. He was a bad person. He was an asshole to me and a monster to all of you." Will swallowed. "I was even going to shoot him myself, given the opportunity."

"He was still your grandfather." Mom touched his cheek. "You go inside. McKenzie, darling, take him inside. Your room is all the way down on the right."

"Thanks, Mom." I slipped out of Will's arms so I could take his hand. I tugged him into the cabin, which was just as rustic on the inside, with exposed, rough wooden beams and it looked like an old-fashioned pump at the sink.

"I've got my doubts about running water," Will said with a slight smile.

"I'm working on it!" Moose called from another room. "We just might not be here long enough to enjoy the fruits of my labor. Depending."

Depending. I looked at Will and tugged him down the hall. "We might be a few—"

"See you at breakfast!" Moose said. "We'll leave your dinner outside the door if you're hungry."

"Thank you." I hauled Will into our room.

It was tiny but cheerful, with one small window, a full-sized bed, and one small dresser with a pitcher, bowl, and bar of soap for washing up. There was a hope chest at the foot of the bed and a happy, floral quilt on the bed itself.

"He's definitely a quilt guy," Will said, running his hand over the quilt on our bed.

I took his hand between both of mine. "I'm so sorry, my love."

He cleared his throat a few times. "It's okay. I meant what I said. I was planning to kill him myself one day."

"Oh." I bit my lip. "Are you feeling like Moose robbed you, then?"

Will barked out a little laugh. "No. Just relieved. It would have been hard to do it myself, despite everything he's done. And I think that makes *me* an asshole, too."

"No! Not at all," I insisted. "He's family. He was your family. It doesn't matter how evil he was, there were always going to be moments when he was actually decent to you. You can't just erase all that by shooting him. I'll bet you're thinking of those times right now."

He looked away. "That's... the problem."

"Of course it's a problem! You're going to miss the good parts of hi—"

"No. You don't understand," he interrupted me. "I can't remember a single time he was encouraging of anything I wanted to do. Proud of any accomplishments I thought were important. Or even just listened to me and my problems. It was always push, push, push. You *will* do this. You *will* do that. You're not working hard enough. When he said he loved me, I knew he didn't mean it. Even as a child." He squeezed his eyes shut. "My grandfather is dead, and I'm not one bit sorry. Does that make me a monster?"

"What?! No!" I hugged him. "That just goes to show what a monster *he* was. He couldn't even get one person to love him and couldn't love his own grandchild. That's just wrong. So wrong. He obviously had no soul."

"That'd be unfortunate because I wouldn't mind imagining him in hell," he said darkly.

"Oka-ay, maybe dial *that* back a little bit, not that I blame you. Or that I won't be imagining the same thing. You know what? Never mind. We'll imagine it together," I responded, playing with the ends of his hair.

Will nuzzled his face into my neck, wrapping his arms around me. "I love you," he murmured against my skin.

"I love you, too," I said desperately.

We stood that way for a long time. Then his hand slid down to my ass. "Should we test how well-made that bed frame is?"

I laughed, then leaned up and kissed him. "Absolutely."

Caleb

"So," I said as Jacey walked into our room. "He's dead."

"Ding-dong?" she replied, leaning over to fluff my pillows.

I kissed her. "I only wish he was the only one we had to worry about. What was with that list the attorney general had?"

"I have a feeling Masterson wasn't alone in his evil scheming. I suspect it must have been some sort of ring." She echoed my thoughts.

"True. Maybe Will knows more about it. He should tell Moose." I stroked her hair as she laid down next to me.

She put a hand on my thigh. "Let them be, for now. I'm sure Will has a lot of complicated feelings about what just happened to Masterson."

"Mine really aren't that complicated. Does Moose have any champagne around here?" I grinned.

Jacey gave me a gentle swat. "We're not toasting his death with Will just down the hall."

"Trust me. Will's about to be a very happy man and isn't going to give a damn what we do down here," I said.

She rolled her eyes. "And just two weeks ago you were lamenting that the two of them fell in love."

"I've changed my mind. He's protective, devoted, strong, and a decent human being who doesn't stifle her," I replied.

Jacey's eyes narrowed. "Were you talking to Shep or Moose?"

Busted. I felt my cheeks heat up. "Moose."

"You should be listening to your wife," she sniffed.

Fuck. I'm in trouble now. "It's just... different between guys."

"Uh-huh." She looked even more pissed off.

I tried something else. "And... you were already such a huge fan I wasn't sure about getting an unbiased opinion...."

She scowled.

"... s-sweetheart..." I gulped.

Jacey sat up. "You know, when you hit China, you're supposed to stop digging."

"I love you," I said. "I wasn't not listening to you, I swear! I just needed a second opinion, that's all."

"China. Stop. Digging," she sighed.

I decided it was probably best to shut the hell up. "I'm sorry."

"No, you're not. But nice try." She perched on the edge of the bed. "You're lucky I love you, Caleb Killeen. I'm very angry with you right now, though."

"I am sorry I hurt you," I insisted. "I really am."

"I know," she replied. "But right now, that's not enough."

Now the chest wound I had was not the only reason my heart was in pain. "Jacey?"

"I've stood by you through all of it. Through everything. But you needed a 'second opinion' from a 'guy'? You don't think I can be 'unbiased'?" She shook her head. "You're being unfair to me and to us as a couple, and you're treating it like it's no big deal. I'm... disappointed, Caleb."

Oh hell. "Boys are dumb?" I tried.

"That's true. But that's not going to save your ass today." She stood and kissed me on the head. "I need some time. I'll be back with dinner."

Fuck. FUCK!!! "Jacey...."

She left, closing the door quietly behind her.

"Sonofabitch!" I threw the blankets off me, intent on going after her. However, my chest screamed in pain when I tried to get out of bed.

I fell back against the pillows, gasping for air. "Jacey."

While I sat there, helpless to do anything but think of what an idiot I was, muffled sounds came through the wall. At first, I wondered if it was Will and McKenzie... getting it on. But then I remembered their room was further down the hall. Plus, I only heard two male voices.

It took me a minute, but I figured out Shep must have been in the next room, and he was talking to Moose.

There was movement, and then suddenly I could hear them more clearly.

"I'm goin' to get your mother back," Moose said, "no matter what it takes."

"She wouldn't want you to do what you're thinkin' of doin'," Shep replied. "When she finds out, she's gonna claw your eyes out."

I had a bad feeling. I scooted to the other side of the bed, earning me more wrenching pain, and pressed my ear to the wall.

"Shep, they're good people. I ain't denyin' that. But I love your mama. And I love you. I don't love them. If that asshole Ike Freeborn will trade for them, then that's what I'm gonna do. You ain't in any fit state to stop me anyhow," Moose explained.

Holy shit! We needed to get out of here, and fast! I pushed off the wall and willed my battered body to get out of bed. I hoped, with enough adrenaline, I could make at least as far as the hallway. I didn't think Jacey had gone far, but if I didn't see her from the door, I could always hobble down to McKenzie and Will's room.

That was the plan, anyway.

With herculean effort, I swung my legs over the side of the bed and slid my feet to the floor. Step one, accomplished.

Then I pushed off the mattress with my fists and forced myself to stand.

Or rather, tried.

My chest screamed in protest, and it knocked the wind right out of me. I tumbled to the floor with a loud thunk, one leg hitting the bed leg. The whole bed frame banged against the wall.

I clutched my chest. The talking had stopped.

Dread rose in me as I heard heavy footsteps coming from the next room up to my door. Like some terrible horror film, the knob on the door slowly turned.

The door creaked open, and Moose stood in the doorway. He frowned down at me. "Caleb, what the hell do you think you're doin'?"

I decided to play dumb. "Jacey and I had a fight. I wanted to go see her."

He raised an eyebrow at me.

I hoped I looked innocent.

Apparently, I didn't. "You been listenin' in on me and Shep?"

There was no way I was walking right into that one. "Why would I?"

"Because you're a suspicious person. Life taught you that." He sighed and sat down on the floor next to me. "You were tryin' to warn the others and escape."

"Warn the others about what? Is there a gas leak or something?" I couldn't see any good coming out of admitting what I knew.

Moose clapped me on the shoulder.

I winced.

"Caleb, you been a good husband and father. Real good protector and provider and all that. But you're a shit liar." He gave me a slow once-over. "Now I need to decide what to do with you."

"How about you realize that everything Masterson has ever touched is poison. You can make a deal with Ike, but he's going to double-cross you. You're going to end up dead, and so are Shep and Dolly. I can promise you that," I said.

Moose shrugged. "This ain't my first rodeo. I know how to handle a hostage exchange."

"Not with these people, you don't." I had to make him understand the cancer Masterson and all his minions were.

"I'm gettin' Dolly back one way or another. But now you're gonna be a problem." He sighed heavily. "I didn't want to have to do this. Not to any of you."

My throat went dry. "Do what?"

He stood, went to the bedside table, and opened the drawer. From inside, he pulled out his kit full of vials and syringes.

"What are you planning to do, Moose?" I asked.

"You just remember, I didn't want to do this," he said again, loading up a syringe from a bottle he'd never used before.

I began dragging myself toward the door, but he blocked me.

"All's that's gonna happen is you're gonna go to sleep," he explained. "You'll just stay asleep. Forever."

I thought of calling for Jacey, but I couldn't bring her into this kind of danger. She'd just become another casualty. And even if Shep wanted to help, he was probably just as bed bound as I was. "*Will!!!*" I yelled at the top of my lungs.

Moose frowned and kicked the door shut. "He can't hear you. They're knockin' boots. And Jacey's takin' a walk outside. I saw her through the windows. So, there ain't nobody comin' to help you."

I grabbed his leg and tripped him.

The syringe went flying.

"Damnation!" He hit the floor hard. The syringe rolled under the bed.

I crawled toward the door, my whole body shaking with pain.

He gripped my ankle and dragged me back. "You'd have been a great soldier in the special forces. But you're near-fatally wounded. You might as well just give up."

"I've *never* given up," I growled and kicked him in the balls.

Moose grunted, but surprisingly, his grip didn't loosen. "Low blow, Caleb."

"Hey, like you said, I'm wounded," I replied.

He hauled me across the floor and knelt on my chest.

I'd never felt pain so intense in my entire life. I gasped for air. For relief.

"Don't worry. It ain't gonna hurt long." He felt under the bed for the syringe.

"What... does... it... do?" I panted as his arm came back out. The syringe was in his hand.

"Well, I'm givin' you an overdose," he said. "It ain't gonna kill you, but it's gonna make you a vegetable. I need you alive for the trade."

Fear lanced through me. Raw, terrible fear. "Don't."

Moose looked truly regretful. "Sorry. I have to."

"Please." I struggled, but he just pressed his knee down harder. The pain was paralyzing. "Please don't," I said again.

With a shrug, he pushed the needle of the syringe into my neck.

"I'm sorry," he repeated before pressing down on the plunger.

Jacey, was my last conscious thought. *I love you.*

Sign up for my newsletter here: https://subscribepage.io/TfsA3A

www.ingramcontent.com/pod-product-compliance
Lightning Source LLC
Chambersburg PA
CBHW060319310726

48976CB00007B/2383